DATE DUE

AP 21 '05			

GOLDEN GIRL *and other stories*

GILLIAN CHAN

Kids Can Press Ltd.

First U.S. edition 1997

Text copyright © 1994 by Gillian Chan
Jacket illustration copyright © 1994 by Bernard Leduc

Kids Can Press Ltd. acknowledges with appreciation the assistance of the Canada Council and the Ontario Arts Council in the production of this book.

Published in the U.S. by
Kids Can Press Ltd.
85 River Rock Drive, Suite 202
Buffalo, NY 14207

Published in Canada by
Kids Can Press Ltd.
29 Birch Avenue
Toronto, ON M4V 1E2

Edited by Charis Wahl
Interior designed by Tom Dart/First Folio Resource Group, Inc.
Chapter openers illustrated by Kimberly Yuill

Printed and bound in Canada

97 0 9 8 7 6 5 4 3 2 1

Canadian Cataloguing in Publication Data

Chan, Gillian
  Golden girl and other stories

ISBN 1-55074-385-6

1. Children's stories, Canadian (English).* I. Title.

PS8555.H39243.G65 1994 jC813'.54 C94-931475-2
PZ7.C53Go 1994

Contents

The Buddy System *1*

Elly, Nell and Eleanor *17*

Golden Girl *37*

Small-Town Napoleon *63*

Alternative Measures *97*

This book is for all those people who made it possible — my parents, Henry and all my "writing" friends.

The
Buddy
System

I've always been surprised that I've had so few problems with school, considering the odds. I'm not boasting, but I'm very smart – "gifted," as my mom describes me to her committee-lady friends – and that doesn't always go down too well. I'm lousy at sports, a real big deal at my school. Still, I suppose growing up in a small place helps. I've known most Elmwood kids my age since kindergarten, and we've had time to get used to each other. I haven't got many friends – hey, I haven't any – but that's fine by me. I'm good at amusing myself. I spend lunch in the library or in Kravitz's science lab – he lets me work there in exchange for looking after the animals. But the real reason I've had it so easy is probably Buddy Covington.

In all those books they have in the library, the ones for "young adults," Buddy and I, the two misfits, would team up and through a series of moving adventures would become loved by one and all. Now you know and I know that's a load of crapola. Kids like to have someone they can pick on. I'm lucky they chose Buddy rather than me. So I keep as much distance between me and Buddy as I can. There's also a practical reason to avoid Buddy. He stinks – a ripe odour of unwashed body, dirty clothes and farmyard.

Buddy's the last Covington in the school and looks as if he might be the first one to actually graduate. His five brothers all dropped out as soon as they were old and big enough to work on the family farm. Buddy's no smarter – he's probably the dumbest of the lot – but he's so scrawny and sickly that he'd be no use on the farm. He always seems to have a cold, and his eyes are red and watery, crusted with mustard-yellow goo that clumps round stiff white eyelashes. I feel kind of sorry for him because he's so dumb that it's easy for the kids to set him up so he makes a fool of himself or, better still, loses his temper. Then you can sit back and watch the tears and snot explode as he yells incoherently.

But their teasing was pretty harmless – it wasn't like they physically hurt him or anything – and I had this feeling that maybe Buddy even enjoyed it a little. At least someone was paying him some attention, which he never got from his five hoglike brothers.

Then Bob Lowther arrived. It was late January, one of those bleak, grey days when snow hurled itself against the windows. We were sitting in history class, listening to Lake drone on and praying that the principal would close the school. For a moment, I thought it was going to happen as he peered through the window in the door, but when he came in it was to introduce, "our new classmate who is joining us from Toronto." As he spoke he gestured vaguely behind him, but there was no one there. A glare from Lake stopped our sniggering as the principal dashed back out into the corridor. This time a kid followed him, slouched against the door-frame, a half grin sliding across his face as he surveyed the room. Huffing into his moustache, the principal waved jerkily for the kid to come and stand beside him.

"This is Bob, Bob Lowther. I'm sure you'll make him welcome. Remember, it's pretty hard to come to a new town and a new school."

With a nod to Mr. Lake, the principal was on his way, leaving us to contemplate the new arrival, who continued to look us over with that maddening half grin in place. Now, in those books I told you about, I'd be overjoyed by a chance to make a friend, but there was something about him that made me dread that Lake might send him to the empty seat next to me. I didn't know exactly what it was then. Maybe it was that he seemed so cocky, or maybe it was just the look of him. He wasn't tall but he was stocky, muscular in an almost adult way, with the beginnings of a moustache. He wore tight black jeans, slashed artistically around the knees. Even on such a cold day, he was wearing a thin white sleeveless T-shirt. He did have a jacket, a black denim one, but he carried it over his shoulder, suspended from one finger. The oddest thing was the hat. Not a tuque like the ones we wear to keep warm, but some kind of woollen hat rolled into a sort of rimmed pancake on the back of his head.

"Bob, there's an empty seat there by the window, next to Michael. He'll show you round today and help you sort out your timetable."

I was safe. I should have known that Lake wouldn't risk putting the new kid with the class weirdos, that he would choose someone safe – Michael Rizzo was captain of the football team, Mr. Clean-cut, but he's OK. He's not a dumb jock and he's never given me any trouble. We've even worked together on a couple of assignments when some teacher has put us together.

Bob started to saunter down the aisle to the seat that Lake had indicated but stopped and turned around when Lake spoke again.

"Bob, one small thing. We don't usually wear hats indoors here." That was typical of Lake. Forget the fact that it was the guy's first day and you're showing him up in front of all these new people, just so long as you prove you're in control.

Bob's grin broadened, and with an elaborate gesture he removed the hat and stuffed it into his back pocket where it stuck out like a tongue. "No problem." His voice was husky and amused.

I found it hard to concentrate after that. Lake's never exactly interesting and he was going over the causes of the Second World War. My dad's a history buff, so I've been reading about this stuff since I was nine or so. I kept sneaking looks back at the new guy. We were meant to be taking notes as Lake droned on, but Bob sat slouched in his chair, staring around the room. The hat was back on his head.

At first he was quiet about not doing any work in class. He'd pick up his pen when he was told to and then put it down again as soon as the teacher's attention was somewhere else. After about two weeks, though, it seemed to be his mission to make sure that no one else did any work either. It took Miss Grainger, our English teacher, two lessons to realize that our jumpiness and twitching were caused by Bob scoring direct hits with spitballs or lighted matches. She stalked over to his desk. "That's enough. Go to the principal's office and wait for me there."

Bob leaned back so his chair balanced on two legs and smiled up at her. "Why?" he asked very politely. "What have I done?"

Miss Grainger seemed taken aback. She wasn't used to kids questioning her or giving her trouble. "You know why, Bob. Just go. I'm not going to tolerate this kind of childish behaviour."

Bob continued to smile but his voice was flat. "No. I won't."

This shocked us all. Miss Grainger went white. We heard the quaver in her voice, although she tried to control it. "We won't waste any more time on this. I shall be reporting your behaviour and insolence, Bob."

The lesson degenerated into a holding pattern until the bell went. Bob didn't throw any more spitballs or matches. He just grinned at Miss Grainger every time her eyes skittered to where he lounged in the corner.

Bob varied his tactics for each teacher. With Kravitz, our biology teacher, it was psychological warfare. Whenever Kravitz started to talk there would be this thin humming, like a trapped mosquito. Kravitz took to pacing the classroom, trying to identify the source of the noise. Once, Bob held it a second too long.

"So, the gentlemen at this bench," said Kravitz. "Which of you is it? You, Lowther?"

"Me?" Bob looked like an altar boy accused of stealing from the collection plate.

"Yes, you. We never had this problem until you graced us with your presence." Kravitz was looming over Bob.

"Why do you always pick on me? You teachers are all the same."

Kravitz just pursed his lips and then resumed his lecture. As soon as he turned away from Bob's bench, the humming started again. I could have sworn, though, that this time it was Mark Lister, who was sitting next to Bob. Kravitz launched himself at the bench. Grabbing Bob by the shoulders, he lifted him out of his seat and pushed him towards the door. Kravitz is a big guy and in full rant is very scary, but Bob went out yelling and protesting. "You all saw that. You're witnesses. I wasn't doing anything and he grabbed me. I'll have him up for assault! My mother's got a friend who's a lawyer."

Bob's mother did show up, but not to complain. It seemed as if she was always sitting outside the principal's office, pale and tired. She seemed young for a mother, dressed in denim and wearing all this ethnic jewellery. She spent hours with the principal and the guidance counsellor. Rumour had it that she used to cry, that she didn't know what to do with Bob. How it was all his father's fault — his new wife couldn't stand Bob, so he'd been sent here to live with his mother.

My early fascination with Bob was turning to irritation and fear. Irritation because, apart from French and physics, Bob was in every one of my classes and teachers spent their time trying to maintain order rather than teaching. Fear for two reasons. I figured that once the novelty wore off, people would get tired of his antics, but for at least half the class, he became a kind of hero. It was as if there had been an underground river of violence and anarchy that Bob had found. Some copied his style of dress, even down to the hat, and tried to behave like him too, mouthing off, refusing to work and making a nuisance of themselves. The other thing that scared me was that he was a bully.

No, wait — Bob made bullying an art form. There was a playful slap that was just a little too hard or a verbal grinding down. His behaviour had an unnerving randomness about it — no one was safe — and it was impossible to predict how long any personalized terror campaign might run — a day or weeks.

At first, he practised on the kids in the lower grades.

"Hey, kid, what are you staring at? Yeah, you, the ugly one with the blue sweatshirt." His tone was challenging and you knew that any answer would be a wrong one.

"Nothing."

"Did you all hear that? The little toe-rag just said that I'm nothing. Come here." The grin permanently glued to Bob's face would become huge as he drew near the victim. If he was caught, his innocent act was always convincing.

"Just a bit of fun. Didn't mean to hurt him. Are you OK, kid?"

He would even lash out at his followers. It was little wonder that my bowels churned every time he so much as looked in my direction. I've all the qualities and weaknesses that would make any self-respecting bully's mouth water. It seemed only a matter of time before he would focus on me. I went through each day with my stomach in knots, waiting for the first gibe. So Buddy Covington's return to school after being absent since the day after Bob's arrival seemed like a miracle. It was obvious that he would be Bob's next victim.

Buddy had been away because his perpetual cold had turned into bronchitis. When he came back he looked worse than ever – thinner, with a greyish cast to his skin and a cough that made his whole body shake like a car whose engine wouldn't start. Not one day passed before Bob started in on him.

In the cafeteria line, Bob turned to Mark Lister, already a dedicated follower. "What's that stink?"

Mark never catches on quickly. "I don't smell anything.

What do you mean?"

Bob grinned. "You can't smell it? It smells like pig crap and it's coming from behind us."

Mark looked around, still not getting it. I knew, though. Buddy was standing a few kids behind them, looking vacant.

"Hey, you! You stink! What do you do, wallow with pigs before school?"

Buddy tried to pretend he was not being spoken to and looked vaguely around.

"Yeah, you snot-face, I'm talking to you." Bob moved in closer, jabbing Buddy in the chest. "I said, you stink. I don't want you near me. Go to the end of the line where you won't spoil everybody's appetite."

In a moment of rare bravery, Buddy quietly said, "No, I don't have to do what you say." He looked around, trying to make eye contact, but everyone looked down or away.

Bob's face flushed. He started jabbing Buddy harder, punctuating each shove with "I said, move!" He finally sent Buddy sprawling into a nearby table.

Buddy came up sobbing and charged Bob, head down, arms flailing. Bob held him off easily, a satisfied smirk on his face as he turned towards Mark, waiting for him to applaud his leader.

Buddy spluttered, screaming, "My brothers ... they'll ... b –" Buddy's last word was lost as Bob caught him square on the nose, causing a spurt of blood to mingle with the tears and snot on Buddy's face.

The noise forced Lake, who was eating his lunch, to stop pretending that nothing was happening and come over. He looked with distaste at Buddy, who had already launched into his story. "Yes, Covington, they always pick on you, don't they? It's never your fault. Just stop snivelling. Now someone tell me what happened. Calmly."

Bob, eyes fixed on Buddy, said, "It was an accident. I turned around to talk to Mark and this kid bumped into me and fell. When he got up, he started hitting me, sir. I tried to hold him off but he went crazy. I only hit out the once and that caught his nose. I didn't mean to hurt him." Bob's eyes flickered towards Mark.

Mark picked up the cue. "That's how it happened. You know what Buddy's like, Mr. Lake, getting all worked up like he does."

Lake looked around at the rest of us in the line-up. "Anyone else? What about you, Dennis? You're observant."

I winced, conscious of Bob's unblinking stare and Buddy's hopeful expression, "Er . . . yeah . . . Buddy fell."

That was it. Systematically, Bob set about making Buddy's life more miserable than it already was, and Buddy's old tormentors gained new inspiration. An exaggerated pantomime was performed every time Buddy came anywhere near them. They held their noses, opened windows and made noises of disgust. Bob even produced a can of air freshener from his backpack and sprayed it around ostentatiously. If Buddy touched anything, it was as if it were suddenly radioactive.

Apart from the teachers, no one called him Buddy any more. Bob delighted in thinking up new names for him, and everyone used them, hoping to avoid the same treatment. So Buddy was Crapola, Hog-breath, and Pus-face.

So, what did the teachers do about all this? Well, apart

from Kravitz, who seemed to have cowed Bob, not much. Most of them were having enough trouble just getting through lessons to actually confront Bob. Some, like Lake, had had years of trouble from Buddy's brothers, who were mean as well as stupid, and seemed to take a kind of sick satisfaction in seeing Buddy suffer.

At first, Buddy reacted as usual, sobbing and losing control. Bob loved it. I could see him waiting for Buddy to go for him again so he could really hurt him; but after about two weeks, Buddy's behaviour changed: it was as if he had gone deaf and blind.

Nothing Bob did provoked a reaction. Buddy, his face set like stone, just stared down at his desk.

The Bob clones soon lost interest – it's no fun if your victim won't play the game – but some who had developed a taste for bullying turned their attention to me. They couldn't get me on personal hygiene, but they found other ways.

"Hey, look who's here. It's supernerd. Have we been having a nice little chat with Kravitz?" This was accompanied by a chorus of wet, kissing sounds.

I'm not that well co-ordinated, so they found ways to trip me up or mess up my science experiments by knocking into me. In gym, they found endless opportunities to hit me with balls and bats – and who could say it wasn't my fault, me being so clumsy.

Learning from Buddy, I presented the best stone face I could, and after a couple of days of insults and shoves, they gave up.

Bob was more dedicated. He still concentrated his efforts

on Buddy, even if he had to go it alone, but he became more and more obvious and frustrated in his efforts to make Buddy respond. When words failed, he openly assaulted Buddy, tripping him, shoving him and even punching him. Nothing worked. Buddy would pick himself up and move off. He had taken to smiling slightly on such occasions, which irritated Bob. Some of the kids were starting to cheer Buddy on – from a distance, of course; we weren't suicidal. Once in the cafeteria, as Buddy calmly got up from the floor and methodically cleared up his scattered food, a lone voice called out from the crowd of onlookers, "Way to go, Buddy!" A scattered chorus cheered. Bob's face went rigid and, gathering his cronies, he marched out.

The showdown came in a craft class when Albert, our teacher, said he was going to the office, but we all knew that he'd gone back to sneak a cigarette in the woodwork store. Now it would be nice to say that Buddy was good at woodworking. In those books I was telling you about, the dumb kid is always a fantastic artist or has a great voice, only no one realizes. Yeah, well, Buddy was as useless at woodwork as he was at everything else, but at least he looked as if he actually liked what he was doing.

Buddy had been working for months on the ricketiest rabbit hutch I'd ever seen. He was bending over it, trying to line up the hinges on its sagging door, so he didn't see Bob coming up behind him. Bob swaggered past and lurched sideways as if he had tripped, sending Buddy crashing forward onto the hutch.

"Hey, sorry, an accident." Bob spread his hands in a parody of innocence, struggling to keep his voice serious.

Buddy said nothing. He stared at the wreckage of the hutch for a few seconds, looked down at the splinters stuck to his faded sweatshirt and made a few half-hearted attempts to brush them away. Then Buddy picked up an Olfa knife from the bench and moved towards Bob.

"Come on, I said it was an accident." There was a new uncertain quaver in Bob's voice.

Buddy's silence and expressionless face terrified me. Bob moved backwards, looking frantically around for help. At first no one moved. Then Mark Lister, I think, stuck out his foot so Bob lost his balance and thudded down on his back in the wood shavings and sawdust on the floor. Buddy threw himself on top of him, the knife point at Bob's throat. I could see a bead of blood form and held my breath, knowing with absolute certainty that Buddy would stick the knife in.

"Covington, what the hell do you think you're doing? Put that knife down!" Albert launched one arm and levered him off Bob, who lay there, his face the colour of pond water.

Things happened in a blur after that. Buddy and Bob were hauled away by Albert. Another teacher came and sat with us, ignoring the buzz of conversation. At intervals a messenger came from the principal and bore us away individually to answer questions. I don't know what the others told him exactly, but it must have been pretty much the same as what I told him, as he didn't seem at all surprised by my account of Bob's persecution of Buddy.

I bet you're thinking, here it is, the moral that always rounds off stories like these. You're probably guessing Bob never returned and Buddy was accepted by his classmates and went on to become one of those dumb but salt-of-the-earth characters. Well, I have tried to warn you about setting too much store by what you read. Bob's back, still a pain, even though he's lost his credibility and his followers now prefer their own brand of stupidity. Buddy, well, having discovered what power can do, is working on becoming a thug like his brothers, but he's easy to deal with because he's still a scrawny one. And me? Let's just say I'm still beating the odds.

Elly, Nell and Eleanor

T he metallic sound of my key in the front door makes me shudder. I know she will have heard it. All afternoon, she will have been watching the hands of the clock, although she will pretend that she has been reading the book lying artfully upon her lap.

"Eleanor, is that you?"

I squeeze my eyes tight so that no light gets in. My lips clench, too, imprisoning the words that long to fly out at her. My father is never home before seven, and no one else but me has a key. I stand as still as I can, trying to delay the moment that I must face her.

"Eleanor" – the voice is pitched high, irritable – "what *are* you doing out there?"

I try to relax, place my books carefully on the ornate hall table, take off my coat and scarf and hang them neatly in the closet. In the mirror above the table I look as if I am under water, my pale skin grey and my long, fair hair like limp green weeds. I practise the smile I display when I greet her, lift the corners of my mouth, but it doesn't work – there is a hint of a snarl. I won't smile.

I open the front-room door. There she is, sitting on the velvet sofa in front of the television, her ankles neatly crossed, her hands folded on the open book, as if she is posing for a photograph. The folds of her flower-patterned wool skirt are carefully arranged. She pats the space next to her and I see the dust motes dance.

"Come and tell me about your day. You're late." Her smile is still in place, but the eyes glitter. One hand strays to the collar of her sweater, and she straightens it, flat and perfect. "I have told you so often, Eleanor, that you are not to hang around the variety store after school. It gives such a bad impression."

A bubble of laughter rises in my throat, and I cough to cover it. I have never "hung around" with others after school. It is a fiction that Mother likes to maintain as no one ever calls me. Nor do I ever visit friends. I keep my voice neutral, to head off the familiar complaints that will come if I do not give the correct response. "I didn't hang around, Mother. I stopped at the pharmacy to buy the cream that you wanted. You asked me to this morning."

A flicker of what might have been anger crosses her face. I can see the network of wrinkles on her cheeks, the heavy coating of powder trapped in the crevices and the fine hairs.

"Don't stand there like that, Eleanor, you look so gawky. A lady should never draw attention to herself. Sit down and tell me about school." She smiles again, tremulously but bravely. "You know how lonely I get here, with no one to talk to all day. I don't meet other people as you and your father do."

My stomach knots and I suppress the urge to shout at her that her loneliness is of her own making. There is nothing wrong with her, no reason why she should not go out. If I pointed out that our house is no more than a ten-minute walk from the shops, the library, she would look pained. Then she would patiently explain how provincial she finds Elmwood, how uncultured the people are, how much better things were back home in England. After twenty years here, she still calls England home. I have never been there. Elmwood is all I have ever known and I like the people here. They're open and kind and I can pretend that I do not see the pity in their faces as they speak to me.

I sit down in the armchair across from her. She smoothes her hand across the seat next to her but says nothing. I lean back, willing my muscles to relax, untwisting my fingers and making them lie straight in my lap. Where should I start? Her version of my school life is coloured by the stories she tells of boarding school in England: gymslips, prefects, jolly hockey sticks and midnight feasts in the dormitories. It is a source of shame that I do not go to a private school, and a bludgeon against my father. Not only did he take her away from England but he cannot keep her in the style that she claims to have grown up in. He never contradicts her, but he smiles ruefully when he describes how, on his only business trip abroad, he struck up a conversation with the young woman eating her sandwich in the park near his hotel, how eager she was to show him around London, to quit her job in the library and leave her drab bedsit to be swept into marriage and a new life in Canada. He told me how they married in a registry office: one witness a business colleague of his, the other a complete stranger dragged in from the street. Mother invited no one.

"Eleanor, I'm waiting."

"Oh, it was the same as always. I got an A on my English essay."

She pounces on that. "You take after me in that respect, thank goodness. Sometimes I think your father is barely literate."

I must dam it, the flow of criticism. "We have a math test on Monday."

"Maths, Eleanor, or mathematics. How many times must

I tell you. 'Math' is so sloppy, so North American."

"Maths, then." I cannot give it her high-flown twist, the perfect enunciation that she does, but she smiles encouragingly at me and waits for me to continue.

"Bob Lowther came back to school today. After his suspension."

"Suspension? He's that new boy, isn't he? What did he do? I don't recall your telling me anything other than mentioning his arrival."

"I did, Mother." I try to hide the small smile that wants to work its way onto my face. She hates to be corrected. "You remember, he got into a fight with Buddy Covington." That hardly does it justice – Bob's reign of terror, his systematic bullying, the shock when Buddy finally turned on his tormentor – but it is enough to set her off, to buy me time to think.

"Well, it is only to be expected. The Covingtons – they're all brutes. And this Bob Lowther – one has to only look at his mother to see what's wrong with the boy, with her hippie ways. He doesn't even have her surname, for heaven's sake." She's like a terrier worrying a meaty bone, enjoying each grisly morsel.

"Mother!" My tone is sharper than I intended. I lock my fingers together and modulate my voice. "Bob has his father's name, that's all. His mother uses her own name, the one she uses professionally."

"Professionally!" The scorn etches its way delicately across her face.

I am always amazed that despite her avowed contempt for Elmwood and its inhabitants, she has so much information about them. She interrogates my father and me each day, but she knows things we don't. The only person she talks to, long phone calls when business is slow, is Miss Jenkins at the library. She pretends they discuss only books. I think of her as a spider, crouched in the centre of a web, her eyes gleaming as she reels in little nuggets of gossip.

I babble on about school, about the principal's new dress code, anything to stop her contempt, her endless judgements, but I am running out of safe things to say. I cannot tell her about Anna Murphy's party and most certainly not about Dennis.

Anna Murphy is having a seventeenth-birthday party tonight. She did not invite me. I am too different, too old-fashioned: the long skirts; the neat pastel blouses and the hand-knitted cardigans. The other girls are not deliberately unkind, just indifferent. I have refused too many invitations, knowing that I must get home because Mother will be waiting. I do not fit into their conversations easily, so they have come not to include me. When I was younger, I used to have friends: differences don't show so much then. I even invited some to come home, but Mother would study them, storing up things to comment on and criticize once they left.

"I know it's unkind to mention it, but Donna has a very coarse way of speaking, don't you think, Eleanor? I do hope you won't emulate her, not after I have spent so much time ensuring that you speak properly. And her table manners, you'd think she'd been half starved! I blame her parents, of course."

I was always at a loss when she did this. I wanted to

defend my friends, knew that my silence betrayed them, hated my complicity in her judgements, but if I protested I knew that I would be forbidden to see them again. They were a bad influence on me – just look at the way I was arguing back.

Other children found my mother odd, even frightening. I remember one asking, "Why's your mother so old? She's like a witch, the way she stares at us." For most, one visit was enough. They would always have excuses not to come again, and I'd catch them looking at me strangely. The friendship would wither away.

No, Anna would never invite me to her party, but Dennis did. And that is the difficulty.

Mother is suspicious of the girls at school, but boys – they are her greatest fear. Every day she warns me about them, that sex is all they are after. Face wrinkled in distaste, she mouths the word "sex" as if to say it aloud would pollute the atmosphere. I often wonder how she and my father produced me, the child of their middle age. She shudders if my father accidentally brushes against her.

Dad says he has to work such long hours, but there are other times when he chooses not to come home. Once I was in town, going to Gagnon's store to buy the English marmalade that Mother likes. Glancing in the window of The Coffee House, I saw him sitting with a woman. He reached out to her, covering her hand with his. She wasn't beautiful or young, but she was laughing, and she put her free hand on top of his. My mother never laughs; my father's jokes make her wince. "Tom, must you always be so loud, so vulgar?" she says, her voice tight.

Mother's fears about boys have always seemed laughable to me. Except for Dennis, boys act as if I am invisible. This year, Mr. Kravitz assigned us to be lab partners. We both knew why. It was his kindly attempt to save us from the embarrassment of being the only ones left after the normal picking and choosing of partners. Dennis is so clever that it scares most people. We didn't talk the first week, risking glances at each other only when we thought that the other was not looking. The work was not too hard and I kept up with Dennis, surprising him, I think. Gradually we began to talk to each other – about the lab work. I don't think that he thought of me as a girl at first, because he gets spectacularly tongue-tied and blushes when any other girl speaks to him. He's quite attractive in a studious, bespectacled way, but this doesn't seem to have occurred to him.

"Why don't you make the tea, Eleanor?" The voice sounds frosty, the words carefully enunciated. "Surely something else of interest must have happened. You can tell me about it while we have our tea."

My lapse into silence has irritated her. I will be careful to make the tea exactly as she likes it, making her work for her revenge. I follow all her rituals: warming the pot; precisely measuring the tea, one spoonful of tea per person and one for the pot; the embroidered cloth on the tray, and the bone-china cups and jug. I know that I have done it faultlessly, but I cannot concentrate because my mind keeps replaying the events that led up to today, and the party.

On Monday, Dennis found me in the library and came and sat down next to me. I knew that something was different. His eyes kept sliding away from mine, locking on to the posters of authors that decorate the walls. "Er, hi, Elly." He kept running his hands through his hair, making it to stick up at wild angles.

"Hi." I did not know what to say, he seemed so agitated.

"Elly?" A wash of crimson surged up his face.

"Yes?" I knew that I was not helping, but he was making me nervous.

"It's about Anna's party on Friday."

Now I knew. He was embarrassed because he had been invited and I had not. I started to speak, to tell him that it was all right, but he raised his hand to stop me.

"I'd like you to go with me." This simple sentence was delivered quickly, the words running into each other, almost as if he had learned it by heart.

"She hasn't asked me, Dennis. I can hardly go to a party I haven't been invited to, can I?" Looking back, I feel so obtuse.

"No, I know, but she asked me and she said I could bring a date."

It still didn't make sense. My voice sounded shrill, incredulous. "Dennis, are you asking me out, to go with you to Anna's party?"

Fooled by my tone, Dennis started to bristle. "Well, if you don't want to go with me . . ."

"No — yes." I felt embarrassed and excited. "It's not that. You took me by surprise, that's all." I took a deep breath. "I'd love to go with you. It's just that nobody has ever asked me out before!"

Dennis smiled with relief. "Elly, you're not supposed to say things like that. You're supposed to be cool. But, well,

I was nervous because it's the first time I've asked anyone out, like to go somewhere out of school." He was waving his hands, excited and triumphant. "I practised in front of the mirror for hours last night." His face grew serious. "Look, I know you said yes, but what about your parents? Will they let you go? My dad says that I can have the car, so I can pick you up and bring you home."

I had told Dennis enough that he knew Mother might present problems, but even if I had said nothing, he would have known what she was like. I knew that people talked about her, how peculiar and difficult she was.

"I'll work something out with my dad. It's probably best not to tell Mother. Otherwise she'll only fuss and think of reasons why I can't go." I would not admit, even to myself, how hard it would be, but I knew that this was a chance – to be normal, to fit in. I could not let it escape.

"Eleanor, surely that kettle has boiled by now?"

I have to keep her calm. I pour the water into the teapot and check that everything is in place before I push the door open and re-enter the living room – the "lounge," as Mother insists on calling it.

She is standing at the window, holding up the net curtain and peering down the street. "I wonder if your father might not be home soon. He certainly went to work very early this morning, and in such a temper, too, rushing out of the house without even bringing me my tea."

"He said that he might be." I try to stop my voice from sounding smug. "His last appointment was cancelled." He promised me that he would be early, but I cannot tell her that. I cannot tell her that he is going to ignore her protests, her tears, and will drive me to the bus station, where Dennis will be waiting. We will not tell her that, of course; we shall maintain the fiction that I am working on a project for history with a school friend. She will still cry and fuss about how selfish we are to leave her alone when she has been by herself all day. I set the tray down carefully on the coffee table.

She turns from the window and comes over to the sofa. "Oh, well, I'm sure that you won't mind keeping me company until it's time to prepare dinner. All I long to hear is another human voice." She pours the tea, one finger lifted delicately from the pot's curled handle.

My fingers lock together, the pressure making my knuckles white. "I've got quite a lot of homework, Mother."

"An hour won't hurt, will it?" Her voice is sugary, wheedling. "I get so bored with just my books and the television. If your father is early, you can do your work after we eat. Talk to me."

She has trapped me. I cannot tell her my plans, not without Dad to back me up. When she weeps I hate it. I want to tell her that I am sorry I have caused such distress. She knows the power of her tears. I cover up these thoughts with chatter, trivial things about school. How Mr. Green wants to set up a school newspaper and has advertised for volunteers for the editorial board.

"That would mean staying after school, wouldn't it?" Oh, she is sharp. "You wouldn't have time. You have the shopping to do before you help me with supper." Her voice is flat. This is a statement that brooks no argument.

I am ashamed that my voice quavers when I answer. "No.

I'd never be chosen. He'll choose someone popular who'll be able to get the other students interested and involved. You needn't worry."

"You make me sound selfish, Eleanor. You know I want you to enjoy yourself, but I really don't think that you would gain much from such an experience. From what you've said, it will be run entirely the wrong way, attract the wrong sort of people. After all, what has being popular got to do with running a newspaper?" She's pleating the fabric of her skirt between her fingers and she stares at me, daring me to contradict her. "It's like so many of these projects at your school, half baked and designed to please the students rather than educate them. You're much better off spending your time here with me. Why, only today Miss Jenkins commented on how mature and responsible you are, how you are a credit to me."

I look down, stare into the dregs of my tea, not wishing to see the look of self-satisfaction that I know will be on her face. My voice is abrupt when I speak, but she does not notice. "Hadn't we better start getting dinner ready, in case Dad is home early?"

She looks around at the lengthening shadows and switches on a small table lamp before sweeping into the kitchen. I trail behind her.

My fingers move mechanically, peeling and chopping the carrots. My mind is with Dennis, remembering how nervous he was, how his hair stood up in crazy tufts. I want to smile when I think that he has actually asked me out, but I don't. There is no need. He asked me; nothing can alter that. Mother keeps up a flurry of questions as she prepares a shepherd's pie, digging away about school, about the school newspaper. I try to answer, but my answers are short. I cannot concentrate.

Once the pie is in the oven, she dismisses me. "You might as well go and start your homework now." And then the little dig: "I obviously bore you."

"No, you don't." I feel obliged to say it. "I really do have a lot of homework and I need to study for the maths test." I resent the way I am making excuses.

Mother pushes her hair from her forehead. In the heat of the kitchen, one curl has had the temerity to escape her rigid, lacquered style. "It's all right. I know that school is important." The words are right but the tone is wrong. I want to say that I'll stay. "You go ahead. I'll watch some television until your father gets back. There must be something interesting on by now."

My room seems odd. I feel out of place. I trail my fingers along the elaborately carved surfaces of the highly polished furniture, breathe on it to obscure my face in the mahogany. Everything is her taste. I long for the clean lines of the furniture I see in catalogues, rooms that look young and lived in. Only the books are mine: school textbooks stacked neatly, chaotic piles of fantasy paperbacks that Dennis has lent me. When I am doing her errands, I sneak time to visit the book shop and linger over the books, touching their bright covers, but with no allowance I cannot buy any.

The door of the wardrobe sticks as I pull it. Inside, the "good" dresses she has made me hang limply, demure floral prints with starched lace collars. Dennis wouldn't notice, let alone care what I wore, but I want to be like the other girls. I know what they wear when they go to parties – they talk in the washroom – the short skirts, the jeans. I had money that Dad sneaked me on my birthday last week, hidden inside the pages of the dictionary that was my official present from him. It was easy to buy a pair of jeans and a T-shirt and smuggle them into the house, hiding the plastic bags with their bright logos behind my sweaters. Sometimes I lock my door and try them on, smiling at the strange girl who stares back at me. That Elly will have friends and will have fun. Emptying the books from my school bag onto the bed, I retrieve my new clothes and pack them carefully inside the bag.

It was Dad who suggested we lie to her, tell her that I am going to a friend's house, the mythical friend with whom I am working on the history project. That would be bad enough. If she knew about Dennis and Anna's party, there would be a scene so awful that it makes my hands sweat even to think about it. That's why I don't want Dennis to come here, even though he offered, said that he would help me face her. I told him that Dad would bring me to the bus station and I could change there. Dennis will wait. He understands.

Dad understands too. "Let's not make life more complicated than it need be, Nell. We both know that your mother would have hysterics if we told her about a party. But don't you worry. I'll drive you to meet your friend, and we'll take it from there," he said. He laughed then, seeming almost to enjoy our intrigue. "It's about time you got out and enjoyed yourself like a normal teenager, eh? You spend far too much time cooped up in this house with your mother. I know I should be home more, but it's not always easy." He had put one arm around my shoulders and hugged me. "You know, Nell, you can always rely on your old dad."

The room is almost dark. I switch the light on and check my watch — almost seven o'clock. Dad is late.

I did not see him this morning. He won't have forgotten, though. Last night, he pinched my cheek, winked and said, "Mum's the word, eh?"

My door opens. "Eleanor, I don't know where your father has got to. Are you sure that he said that he would be early? I think you and I had better eat before supper spoils. I'll keep his warm."

He promised. He would not let me down. Something must have happened. He'll be here soon and I'll still be able to meet Dennis at eight-thirty as planned.

"OK, I'll finish tidying up and then I'll be down." Her mouth twitches at the "OK," but she lets it slide. She must be worried. A prickle of fear works through my body.

Dad's place setting dominates the table as we eat. We both keep glancing at it. Mother looks at the clock, talking constantly, a bright, forced stream of stories that I have heard before. I don't have to answer, just look interested, in spite of thoughts of Dennis and the party. I wonder what the reaction will be when he arrives with me. He is isolated by his cleverness, but he is included more than I am. Will this be enough to get the others to accept me, too? I do not let myself wonder where Dad is.

Mother is looking at me expectantly. She must have asked a question. I stare blankly and she repeats what she said with no admonition for my inattentiveness. "I said, I'm beginning to worry about your father."

I realize, with a sick feeling, that while I was locked in my dreams, the hands of the clock have moved inexorably. It is almost eight. I hold on to the edge of the table.

"Do you think I should ring the police? He did say he was going to be early, didn't he? He may have had an accident. The roads can be very treacherous at this time of year and you know how your father drives." She is scared, but the urge to criticize, to hurt, is too much a habit.

"No." I sound abrupt. "They'd laugh at you. Perhaps a late appointment was scheduled after all." I relax a little. This is what must have happened. "The police would think you were overreacting. He'll be here soon or he'll call."

We pass the rest of the meal in silence. My throat has closed up. I push the food around my plate, creating patterns with my fork in the mashed potatoes. The bus station is on the edge of town. Without Dad, I have no way of getting there. Dennis lives in one of the outlying villages. There is no point calling him – he will have left already. My heart seems to be beating slowly, as if it is turning to stone. In my head, I keep saying, Come on, Dad, you promised. Don't let me down.

We give up the pretence of eating and clear up. I nearly drop a plate, and Mother looks sharply at me. "Let's watch some television, Eleanor" is all she says. "It will help keep our minds off your father's lateness."

It does not. We sit there, the bright colours of some *National Geographic* program swirling about, but neither of us is watching. She keeps looking at the door, and I think of the clothes in my school bag upstairs. The numbness is spreading from my heart throughout my body. I do not allow myself to think of Dennis. At eight-thirty, I find myself biting my knuckles, watching the screen with a hard-eyed intensity that sees nothing.

By the time the phone rings at nine, my mother is twisting her handkerchief between her fingers. She rushes into the hall. "Oh, Tom, thank goodness you've rung. Eleanor and I were beginning to worry." Her voice sharpens, becomes shrill and accusatory. "Where have you been? Your supper is ruined, of course!"

His reply is lengthy, and she says nothing.

I watch her through the frame of the doorway. She is standing so still. I get to my feet. I want to scream down the phone, Where are you? You promised! like a kid denied a treat.

Finally she says, "I see." Her voice is flat and her face shows no emotion as she turns to me in a stiff, awkward movement. "Your father wants to talk to you, Eleanor."

I raise my hand to take the phone, and then realize that I have formed a fist so tight that when I unlock my fingers I can see the indentations of my nails in my palm. She remains standing by the phone and I have to ease past her. "Dad?"

"Nell?" He must be drunk. His voice is slurred and sounds miles away. "Nell, I've got to do it now. I don't think I'll ever have the courage again. You know I wouldn't unless I had to, don't you? It's Julie."

I am hearing what he's saying but nothing makes sense. Who is Julie?

"Julie says I've got to make a decision, got to choose. You'll see. Things will work out."

I wait for him to tell me that he is on his way home now,

and that we'll make it, that Dennis will be waiting for me.

"I'm leaving, Nell. I'm not coming home any more. It's no life putting up with her whims and fancies all the time."

I have become a statue.

"Nell? Nell?" He is shouting. "Are you listening, Nell? I've had a few drinks, sure, but I know what I'm doing. Look, don't worry about anything. I'll send money. Just look after your mother for me. I'll be in touch, give you my new address. Maybe you could come and visit us. I know I can rely on you." He sounds like he is crying. "Nell? Nell, are you still there?"

I let go of the phone and it bounces on its cord.

Tears are running down Mother's face but she tries to smile. "What did I tell you, Eleanor? Never trust a man — they'll always let you down. We'll be fine together, just the two of us."

I picture the bus station — Dennis sitting on a bench, his hands in his pockets against the bite of the wind. His eyes are fixed on the doorway. He walks over to the bank of phones and dials a number, shaking his head when all he gets is a continuous busy signal. He looks at his watch, then walks to the parking lot. He sits in the car for what seems a long time before driving off into the darkness.

I feel as if I am choking.

Golden
Girl

I worked hard to be Anna Murphy's best friend. Don't get me wrong — it was worth it. Without Anna I'd have been nobody. But Anna never has to work hard. She's probably the best-looking girl in town and, what's worse, it's all natural. Even as a little kid she had everyone drooling about how cute she was, with her long blond curls and big brown eyes. Now everyone's telling her she should be a model. They make me want to throw up. She has this fake, modest smile and a "What, me? I'm not pretty enough" routine, and then just eats it up when they all rush to contradict her.

Her dad's loaded, and nothing's too good for "Princess." Boys fight over her — like, actually fight. I used to hope that some of whatever she has would rub off on me. I mean, I deserved some pay-off for all the crap she dished out.

The latest load started the day we went into English class and Miss Grainger had this guy with her. He was drop-dead gorgeous, like one of the hunks we drool over in those magazines we don't admit reading because they're not cool. He was about six foot two with these amazing shoulders. At first I couldn't see his face because he was bent over, reading some list on Miss Grainger's desk. Then, wow! Green eyes with long, thick lashes. Tanned skin without a zit in sight. He even had a slightly crooked nose that saved him from being a total pretty boy.

Anna gasped. "Donna, who *is* he?"

Like I'm supposed to know?

"Aha! Even Grainger's making eyes at him, the dirty old lady." Anna's had it in for Miss Grainger since last year. Grainger just hadn't heard the news that Anna was Miss Perfect and had told her it was a shame that she did just enough work to get a decent grade when if she worked hard she could be brilliant at English. That's a real no-no, criticizing Anna. After all, her entire life the rest of the world's been telling her how wonderful she is.

"Come on, settle down. We've got a lot to do today." Grainger gave some latecomers the death stare as they stumbled in, banging against chairs. "This is Mr. McCallum from the university. He's going to be with us for the next two months. At first he'll be sitting in on some classes, and later he'll be teaching."

Anna, always the drama queen, buried her face in her arms. "Oh no, he's a student teacher. Let's hope he's a keeper. I'd *really* like to get to know him." This last bit came out in the breathy voice Anna uses when she's trying to sound sexy but sounds like she's having an asthma attack. "I hope that creep Lowther doesn't screw things up again."

Anna has this seriously selective memory. OK, Bob Lowther did start the trouble with the last student teacher. She was so stupid. She told us to express ourselves any way we liked. So he did. For Bob, jumping from desk to desk hooting like a chimp expressed exactly how he felt about her dorky ideas, and the rest of us weren't far behind. Anna and I sat on our desks screeching as loudly as we could. A bunch of kids at the back lit up cigarettes. Even Dennis Mason was winging paper planes around. You should have seen his face when one of them hit the student teacher smack between the eyes, and she started to cry. He rushed up to her, apologizing like crazy. Anna was laughing hysterically. And she even gave Elly Kovacs a hard time for about a week afterwards for helping Dennis get the stupid cow out of the room. Here

Anna was blaming Bob for the whole thing, right? Like she was a total angel.

Miss Grainger showed Mr. McCallum to a chair and turned her attention back to us. "Get out your copies of *Julius Caesar* and let's make a start."

Anna was trying to check out the student teacher without being too obvious, so she had made no move to get out her book. I nudged her in the ribs.

"All right, all right!" she whispered, hardly taking her eyes off him as she fumbled in her backpack.

I thought she'd have to concentrate then because Grainger asked her to read Portia. I have to admit it — Anna's pretty good. She's been in just about every school play since kindergarten. When she was a little kid she used to go on about how she was going to be a movie star, but she dropped the idea when Mrs. Snow, our drama teacher, told her how hard it was to break into acting. Now she says she wants to be a news anchor. I can see her doing it, too. Daddy will pay for her to go to some fancy media-studies college. And then she'll waltz up to a television station and expect them to fall all over themselves to give her a job. The sickening thing is that they probably will, because she's good-looking and, no matter how she tries to hide it, pretty smart, too. Me, I'll be lucky to manage a year at the local community college, if I can scrape together the tuition, doing whatever subject is most likely to get me a job, any dead-end job.

"Anna, just what is so fascinating at the back of the room?" Grainger couldn't resist a small smirk when that got a giggle from the class. I pressed my lips together to keep from laughing and put on my best sympathetic face.

Anna just blushed and muttered.

She didn't turn round again after that, but she didn't follow the play either. She had a piece of paper half hidden under her book, and she was doing a pretty passable sketch of McCallum.

"Well, Anna? We're waiting."

Everyone silently turned to look. Anna stared down Miss Grainger with this sneer on her face as if she'd been interrupted at something seriously important.

"It's your line, Anna." Miss Grainger was sounding real snippy. "When you follow the text, it makes it run so much more smoothly for those who *are* listening."

I thought Anna got off easy, but she flounced around in her seat and flicked the pages. She glared at me, and I wasn't much help. I knew the general area, but I'd been too busy watching her to know exactly what speech was next.

"Someone show them where we are, for heaven's sake." Grainger was doing this eyes-rolling-upwards thing she does to show how stupid she thinks you are. It ticked me off that I was being included – I'd been paying more attention than Anna. But that's just typical. Dennis turned around, showing us the page and pointing to Portia's speech.

Anna started reading then. Her face was bright red, and for the first few words her voice was shaky, but she got it together. It was this scene where Portia confronts her husband, Brutus, and Anna had us all believing how angry and hurt old Portia was, even with the geek reading Brutus sounding like a talking log. At the end of the scene, she glared at Miss Grainger.

"There, Anna. See what you can do when you concentrate?"

I thought that was pretty neat, but Anna gave her the hate stare for the rest of the period.

When it was over and Miss Grainger shepherded the student teacher out, Anna packed up her books and turned on me. "What's the matter with you, Donna? You made me look like an idiot back there."

I couldn't believe it. What had I done?

"He'll think I'm a real bimbo, being told off for turning around and then not following the text."

This was my fault?

"You could have just kept track of where we were meant to be." Anna was really getting into it now. "He'll think we're just a couple of airheads."

The self-important, spoiled little creep, pouting because some guy she didn't even know might think she's a ditz. Oh well, all she wanted was someone to lash out at, and guess who was there – good old Donna. I bit back what I really wanted to say, thought it'd be better to suck up to her. That's why she keeps me around, after all. "Come on, Anna, he's got to think you're quite something after the way you read."

That stopped her. "What do you mean?"

"Well, you read Portia like you really felt all those things, so you can't be stupid, right? You must understand the play." I went in for the killer punch. "And I saw him looking at you while you were reading, like he was impressed." I hadn't, of course, but I knew she'd buy it, she's so vain.

"Really?"

"Yeah, really, Anna."

"Come on, let's get some lunch." Anna sauntered out of the room with a huge smile on her face.

This McCallum guy was all Anna talked about for the rest of the day. You'd think he could walk on water, the way she went on. On the way home with some of the others, she was even worse.

"Wow! Is he good-looking – but mature, too."

"Anna, he's probably only five years older than we are," said Michael. "The same age as your brother Liam – and you're always saying what a jerk he is."

Michael was Anna's boyfriend, Mr. Wonderful to her Miss Perfect. They were The Couple, if you get what I'm saying. I suppose it's kind of predictable – captain of the football team and the head cheerleader. I'd kill to get a guy like Michael. But Anna just acted like he was her due or something, and treated him like dirt. All the time, too, not just now going on about how gorgeous the student teacher was, like Michael had no feelings.

I go out with one of Michael's friends on the team, Doug Washburn. He's all right, but that's all. He's OK looking but nothing compared to Michael – Doug looks like those movie actors who play the hero's buddy and never get the girl. I know he has the hots for Anna – what boy doesn't – but he hasn't the nerve to ask her out, so he makes do with me. If I hadn't been Anna's friend I doubt he'd even have bothered. I don't really like him that much but, hey, at least he's on the team.

Anna just stared at Michael like he was stupid. "He's nothing like Liam. You can tell this guy's been around – he's sophisticated."

"Oh, come off it, Anna. You've never even spoken to him, you've seen him once and suddenly you know everything about him." Michael wasn't picking up the danger signals — the way Anna's face was flushing, how her lips were tightening.

"His suit was one of those fancy designer ones — Boss or maybe even Armani," I tossed in to back Anna up, maybe earn back some brownie points.

"So what!" Michael was getting steamed himself now. "Anna, that guy doesn't even know you exist. And even if he does, he's not going to be interested in a schoolgirl."

Anna stopped dead and turned to face Michael. "That's what you think." Giving everyone her biggest, brightest smile, she said, "You just wait and see." Her chin was up, daring Michael to challenge her. What had I started here?

Michael hitched up his backpack. "I'll see you tomorrow. Maybe you'll be in a better mood. Bye, guys." Off he went, not looking back even once.

I'd have been devastated, run after him even, but all Anna did was smile. "I'll show *him*." Looking around, she said, "You'll all see." She linked her arm through mine. "Let's go, Donna. Come over to my house and we'll do our homework." That was a laugh. Anna just wanted me there so she could go on about McCallum. I'd end up doing my homework really late, after I'd watched my kid sisters till my mother got back from work.

By the time Mr. McCallum started full-time at the school, instead of just coming on observation visits, he had a real following, with the girls drooling over him and the boys thinking he was an OK guy because he was a jock and helped out with the sports programs. Anna kept dropping hints that she was going to make a play for him, and she had most people believing she could pull it off. Michael never said anything, just got this closed look on his face. Maybe, if he got really ticked off with her, I could make a move on him.

McCallum's first lesson was OK. At least he tried to make things interesting. Even Bob didn't mess him around. You could tell McCallum was nervous because he was already at the front of the room when we piled in, pacing up and down by the board where he'd written "Living Language." When we actually sat down and showed signs that we'd listen, he relaxed a bit. Anna had bagged some seats right at the front and stared at him like a kid looking at an ice-cream cake.

This "Living Language" crap was all about how language changes. He started off by getting us to work in pairs, writing down as many slang words as we could think of. Bob could really have taken advantage but he didn't, and he had all this great street slang from when he used to live in Toronto. McCallum got all excited, making some crack about how we had a real expert in our midst. Bob almost forgot that he was the school bad boy, and grinned. I could tell that Anna was getting mad, but she had nothing to outclass Bob, so she had to make do with tossing her hair and leaning back so her boobs stuck out. The guys in the front row had a fine time, but McCallum didn't seem to notice. Anyway, by the end of the period she was getting pretty desperate.

It was the homework he set us that gave her a chance to get noticed. He wanted us to talk to someone older, like our parents, and collect a list of the slang they used when they were our age. The idea was that we could see how words had changed, and maybe how some words had different meanings now.

We packed up and I waited like normal for Anna, but she made this sign with her hand that I was to go. I mean, who did she think she was, dismissing me like I'm her slave or something. Michael was starting up the aisle towards her, but I met him on my way out.

"Anna doesn't want us to wait." Well, how else could I say it? He looked as if he might protest, so I grabbed his arm and steered him out of the room.

"What's with her?" Even with the noise in the corridor I could hear how mad he was.

Looking really sympathetic, I said, "Don't worry, Michael. She's talked so much about McCallum that she's got to make him notice her or everyone will laugh at her. Once she's done that, she'll let it drop – you'll see." I was lying through my teeth, of course. I knew how serious Anna was – she'd told me often enough over the past few weeks – but Michael swallowed it.

"Tell Anna I'll be out on the field kicking a football around, OK?"

I was straining to hear what was going on in the room, so I kind of brushed him off. "Yeah, yeah, I'll do that." Once he'd gone, I stood as close to the open door as I could without being seen. Anna was standing by the teacher's desk while McCallum packed up his stuff.

"Mr. McCallum, does it have to be a parent we ask?" Anna was giving him the Smile full blast. It was almost funny to see her run through her tricks.

Without looking up, he replied, "Well, no, anyone older

will do."

"See, I thought I'd ask my great-grandmother." Anna's voice carried real well, all eagerness and please-notice-me. "She's really old, but she's still all there. I visit her every week in the retirement home, and she tells really interesting stories about when she was a girl. She was a suffragette in England." This was a crock. Anna was always complaining about having to visit her, about how she had whiskers and slopped her food.

"That may be too far back, you know. The other kids might find it difficult to relate it to their own experience."

Anna didn't miss a beat. "Exactly. That's why I thought if I interviewed her daughter – my gran – and my own mother, then maybe I could sort of map their experiences, showing how circumstances affected the way they talked and all that." Got him! What teacher wouldn't be flattered by a kid wanting to do extra work for them after their very first lesson? "It would take a long time, but it could be really interesting."

Closing his briefcase, he looked at Anna for the first time. "You're . . . ?"

"Anna. Anna Murphy." She positively glowed.

"Well, Anna, if everyone's as enthusiastic as you are, the next month is going to be fun." He smiled in her general direction and swept out of the room.

I moved well away from the door so Anna wouldn't have any idea I'd seen and heard it all.

"Donna, you were right! He likes me. He was really keen on my idea about the homework and he made a point of asking my name." It all came out in a rush as Anna ran up to where I was lounging against some lockers. Notice the way she just expected me to be waiting, like I had nothing better to do. "This is going to be easier than I thought. You should have seen the way he looked at me." As we passed the glass trophy case, she stopped and checked out her reflection.

I *had* seen the way he looked at her. I didn't say anything – just stored it all away for future use.

Anna made sure she was always the last out of McCallum's class and usually found something to talk to him about. As her best friend, I waited outside in the corridor. It was pathetic, like being back in Grade 3 when you think it's so neat to have a teacher notice you. She gushed away, and he always took time to talk about some assignment or her slang-in-the-family project. She'd actually done the whole thing, just like she said she would – it must have taken her hours. Anyways, pretty soon she'd get him talking about himself. Once she even spun him this line about how English was her favourite subject and how she wanted to be an English teacher. He launched into this long rambling story about how he'd decided on English because he wanted to share his love of literature with kids. If you asked me, it was all a load of crap, but they both seemed to believe it.

I never let on that I listened, just made the right noises when Anna told me her latest triumph – how he looked at her, how he really wanted to ask her out but couldn't because he was a student teacher. It was kind of sad. He obviously liked her, but she was reading far too much into it.

The way Michael acted probably convinced most kids there was something going on. He was so jealous and possessive that if you wanted him to lose his temper all you had to do was say the word "McCallum." There was this dance coming up and Michael practically begged Anna, in front of a whole lot of people, to go with him, like there was a chance she might turn up with someone else. She agreed in this real condescending tone, and when Michael went off, she kind of hinted that he would just be the front to hide what was really going on.

See, the big news about the dance was that McCallum was going to be there. He'd told some guys on the football team that student teachers were encouraged to get involved in the school's extracurricular activities. So, he and the nerdy science type were going to help the regular teachers run the dance. Anna was in heaven.

"This is my big chance, Donna. I know he really likes me but I've got to show him I'm not a kid." She looked like my little sister Stacey does when she watches commercials for real fancy toys on television – she really wants them but is pretty sure she won't get any.

As Faithful Friend, I could dig around a bit, maybe get something I could use on her later. "He knows that already, doesn't he? I mean, the way you say he talks to you when you're alone. You said he just couldn't act on how he felt, that's all."

"Yeah, well, that's true, but I really want to show how different I am from those girls who have crushes on him." She was staring past me, focused on the parking lots. McCallum was walking towards a red sports car. "You know why he was assigned to this school, Donna?"

I didn't, but I knew she was going to tell me.

"He's Warren's nephew."

Typical, Anna calling old man Pelletier by his first name. Apart from Anna's dad, who owns the biggest construction company in Elmwood, Pelletier is about the richest man in town. He has this big poultry-packing factory and a whole load of farms outside town. All I knew about him was that I'd do just about anything not to end up working for him once I was out of school.

"Big deal!"

"My dad says he's staying with his uncle and during the summer he's going to be working up at the processing plant." Anna's voice was quiet and dreamy. It didn't take much to work out what she was thinking. I tried digging a bit more but Anna just smiled real secretively and said, "I'm going to Lexington this Saturday to look for a dress. You want to come?"

Shopping with Anna is not easy, trying to keep smiling while she throws money around like there's no tomorrow and I search for whatever's cheapest but doesn't look too cheesy. "Nah, I've got one already." I changed the subject quick. "What are you looking for?" I didn't want to talk about my dress, a tacky hand-me-down from my cousin, the queen of bad taste.

"Just you wait and see." Anna smiled knowingly and headed off.

Anna wouldn't show me what she had bought until the actual night. Doug and I were going to the dance with her and Michael, so he came by to pick us both up. He didn't ring the doorbell, just honked from the driveway. That was weird, but I didn't say anything when I got into the back seat with Doug.

Anna turned around. "Hi, guys. All set?" She sounded as if she was trying to keep from laughing.

"Put your seat belt on, Anna." Michael's voice was tight. He was sitting up real straight, glaring out the windshield.

"All right, give me a break." Anna stayed twisted, facing us. "He's such a grouch tonight." A giggle escaped, choked off as Michael slammed the car into reverse and backed onto the street so Anna was thrown off balance before she turned and sat facing the front, her seat belt still hanging loose.

"Is your brother the DJ tonight, Anna?" Doug usually has the sensitivity of a bull moose, but I couldn't believe that even he hadn't noticed the tension.

"That's right – Liam's my man." I could have sworn she was still trying not to laugh. Liam was crazy and he'd do just about anything for Anna.

The school gym was already crowded by the time we got there. They'd tried to decorate it with clusters of balloons and paper streamers, but it still looked like a hole. Anna and I went to the cloakroom to take off our coats.

Get this – a deep crimson jersey number that clung to every line and curve of Anna's body. It had one of those necklines that was kind of off the shoulder, and I swear will-power alone was keeping it up.

"Anna!"

Anna spun around to give me the full effect. It was so tight that she couldn't have been wearing any underwear. "Michael doesn't like it." She sounded so smug that I felt real sorry for him.

"It's different." One of my all-time great understatements. She made the rest of us look like little girls in party dresses, all bows and velvet. "What did your parents say?"

"Dad hasn't seen it. He's out with the Rotarians. Mom was OK — just made some crack about borrowing it for the Lions Club dance."

My mother wouldn't have let me out of the house in something like that.

"Do you think *he'll* like it?"

I shrugged. "Hey, what guy wouldn't?"

Walking back through the gym was quite something. Anna kind of glided through the crowd, acknowledging them with smiles and waves, like she was royalty or something. I don't think anyone even noticed me. So, what's new?

Michael and Doug had bagged one of the tables arranged around the walls of the gym. When he saw Anna, Doug went bright red and didn't seem able to speak, which made it real awkward since Michael was sitting there stone faced and silent. Anna and I kept badmouthing everyone around us, why they shouldn't have worn what they did, how badly they'd done their hair — you know, the usual. We didn't really mean anything by it. Besides, Anna's mind was elsewhere. She kept looking around, trying to spot McCallum in the crowd.

"How about dancing?" Anna stood up and looked down at Michael.

He didn't move his eyes in her direction, just shook his head.

Doug found his tongue. "I'll dance with you, Anna."

He didn't even look at me, let alone ask if I minded, and he stepped on my foot stumbling out towards the floor with her. That really showed how I rated.

Michael was white faced. "You said she'd drop it." He

almost spat each word. "She's making a fool of me."

How come I always get it in the neck from everyone? Like it was my fault the way Anna was behaving? "Look, Michael, I was wrong, OK? I think Anna's being a jerk, but I can't do anything about it." I leaned forward and put my hand on his. "I think she's treating you real bad." I waited till he looked at me. "But it's herself she's making look like a fool, not you. People will see through her." I wanted to add it was about time they did but, hey, maybe this wasn't the perfect moment.

He almost smiled. "Thanks, Donna. I really appre – "

"Hey, guys, you should see McCallum. Does he ever look cool." Good old Doug with his usual wonderful timing.

Michael gripped Doug's arm. "Where's Anna?"

"Calm down, she's gone over to talk to McCallum, that's all."

Michael turned. "Do you want to dance, Donna?"

"Sure." I ignored Doug's whining about being left by himself and followed Michael out onto the dance floor.

He headed for the centre of the floor and started dancing, but he was really looking around for Anna. I don't think he'd have even noticed I was there, except that I pointed towards the stage. Anna was with a whole group of girls, clustered round McCallum. She grabbed his hand and started pulling him onto the floor. He glanced back at Miss Grainger, who just shrugged.

Liam was playing a fast number. Anna looked up at him and suddenly the CD stuck. With hardly a pause, Liam had his second player going. His voice came over the loud speaker. "Sorry about that. But never fear, Liam's here. Let's slow the tempo down a bit, get into a romantic mood."

He reached for a switch and dimmed the lights.

In the gloom, Anna threw her arms around McCallum's neck and pressed up against him. His back was rigid and his hands on Anna's waist seemed less holding her than trying to push her away. Even in the dark, they were the centre of attention.

"That's it. I'm out of here." Michael stalked off the dance floor. I headed back to our table so I wouldn't look like a total dork standing there by myself.

"Where's Michael?" Doug asked, a face on him like a spoiled kid.

"Look, I only danced with him because he was upset about Anna." Doug was just dumb enough to believe me. "He saw her dancing with McCallum and took off."

"I'll go look for him," Doug said.

The lights came back up. Anna still had hold of McCallum's hand and he looked real uncomfortable. The dance floor was clearing, and I heard a couple of sniggers as McCallum finally pulled his hand free, muttered something and headed back to Miss Grainger.

For a few seconds, Anna just stood there, looking like a baby whose rattle's been snatched away. Then she lit up a smile and kept it burning all the way back to our table.

"He's the smoothest dancer. Did you see us?" Anna didn't seem to notice Michael and Doug weren't there, just watched closely for my reaction to her next statement. "It's real hard for Iain. He has to play things so carefully till his teaching practice is over. That's why he couldn't dance with me again."

Iain! Right. Like I didn't know she'd made a point of

finding out McCallum's first name from her father. "Yeah, you looked great together." I was more interested in McCallum with Miss Grainger, talking real seriously and looking in our direction.

Finally, it dawned on Anna that I was alone at the table. "He left," I said. "Doug's gone to look for him."

Anna sighed. "He's so immature at times! I mean how are we going to get home?" She sat down, turning towards the dance floor.

Miss Grainger was standing there alone.

Doug never caught up with Michael. He came rushing back, panting. "His car's gone from the parking lot!" He shifted from one foot to the other, like he was waiting for a reward or something.

"He can be such an idiot." Anna was smiling as she said that. It gave her a real buzz to know that she had them lining up for her favours. "Never mind, we'll get a ride with someone else, I'm sure." She was looking around the room, scanning the faces. With a sigh she sat down at the table, picked up her drink and then turned to Doug. "Since everyone seems to have deserted me, how about another dance?"

And that's how I got to spend the rest of the evening, watching Anna make out that she was having a great time. McCallum was nowhere to be seen.

I had to baby-sit the next day. My mom had actually been offered some overtime, which was too rare to refuse. Anna called at nine o'clock.

"Hey, Donna. Do you want to come over?"

"You know I can't leave the brats by themselves."

"But I really need to talk to you." There was a pause. "Can't Stacey watch the little guys? Your mom doesn't have to find out."

"Are you kidding? Stacey would rat on me in a minute. And Mom would murder me if she found out I left Stacey in charge." It would never occur to Anna that she could come over, maybe help me. I have to jump at her command. I think she's been to my place maybe twice, acting like she's doing me some huge favour.

"I wanted to talk about Iain."

I sat down cross-legged on the hall floor, figuring I was going to be listening for a long time. It was weird. I didn't have to say anything, not even make those encouraging "uh-huh" or "mm" noises.

"Oh, Donna, he's got such a great body, all hard and muscular. He smelled good, too, not sweaty. I just know he wanted to say something to me, but everyone was looking at us. He has to be so careful."

What a load of crap.

"Did you see? He didn't dance with anyone else – just me."

I had to face it – she wasn't just doing a number on Michael and the others, she was doing one on herself. Maybe that's what happens when you always get everything you want.

"Monday, I just know he's going to say something." Oh, really? "It's his last week at the school, so he'll be able to take more chances."

Right. I was going to enjoy watching Miss Snot find out how it feels to be disappointed, just like the rest of us. Meanwhile, I'd put up with Anna's hourly calls, saying the same things over and over. And you know what – she never mentioned Michael once.

On Monday, Anna came to school wearing black jeans and boots and a white shirt with a black suede vest over it that cost a fortune. She must have been up real early that morning, because her hair tumbled around her face in that casual way you know takes hours to get right. She was so wired that it was lucky English is always in the morning. I don't think I could have stood much more of did she look OK and what did I think he'd say.

When we got to class Miss Grainger was there, sitting at the back with a note pad. With Anna beside me, it was hard to concentrate. She wasn't really sitting, she was posing. If McCallum asked a question, she just about killed herself to be the one to answer, but he never called on her – not once.

When the period was over, Anna went into her usual routine of packing her things slowly. She was so intent on McCallum that she didn't notice Miss Grainger coming up behind her.

"Was there something you wanted, Anna?" Miss Grainger had to move back to avoid getting stepped on when Anna jumped in surprise.

"Er, I wasn't quite clear about the assignment, that's all." Anna was stuttering. "I, uh, just wanted Mr. McCallum to go over it with me."

Putting her hand in the small of Anna's back, Miss Grainger guided her towards the door. "Ask one of the others. I'm sure they'll have written it down. Look, Donna's over there. Ask her."

Anna's face was brick red.

Miss Grainger came out a few seconds later with McCallum.

As they passed us, Anna turned away, pretending to be looking for something in her backpack. "What's she doing here?" she asked once they'd disappeared down the corridor.

It was pretty obvious to me, but I wanted to see how Anna would explain it away.

"I suppose she has to assess how he's doing, maybe write a report or something." The colour was going from her face now. "Yeah, that's it." She smiled and walked off, the bounce back in her step. "I'll just have to wait, that's all."

The wait was longer than Anna expected. Miss Grainger turned up at every one of McCallum's lessons that week. She even gave up pretending to make notes. I bet most everyone had worked out why she was there. Funny, though. No one said anything to Anna. If it had been me, jokes would have been all over school by now.

Michael hadn't spoken to Anna since the dance, but he and I had talked a few times. He kept saying he hated to see her make a fool of herself. He'd even called me at home once to talk about her. I could get him talking about something else for a bit, make him laugh, but he kept coming back to Anna.

By Thursday, Anna was getting desperate. She couldn't get past Miss Grainger in class, and in the halls McCallum either had people around him or he hurried away from her. She kept telling me he was just being ultra-cautious. Come on! But I could see that she was getting edgy. Maybe this was the time to give Miss Teen Queen a little push, show everybody what an idiot she could be. So I suggested she write him a note.

I was with her when she wrote it, but she wouldn't listen to any of my suggestions. She kept going on about how it had to have the right tone, mature but not pushy, and it took her about a hundred tries to get it right.

Dear Iain,

I know that it has been difficult to balance your role as a student teacher with the friendship that has developed between us. I also realize that you had to treat me like just another pupil. Now that your practice teaching is ending, we can meet as equals. I shall be waiting at The Coffee House on Main Street at 11:00 a.m. on Saturday. No reply is necessary, as I know it might be difficult in the school situation.

Love,

Anna

She got me to leave it on his desk. He plunked his books right down on top of it, so he didn't see it until after all the goodbyes, when he started putting things in his briefcase. For once, Anna didn't hang around, so she didn't see him read the note, make a face and then crumple it up and throw it in the garbage.

Miss Grainger looked at him. "Anything wrong?"

He shook his head and started out of the room. "Nothing important."

After they left, I got the note from the garbage, smoothed

it out and put it carefully in my bag. At least Anna hadn't dotted all the *i*'s with little hearts, but "the friendship that has developed between us" – who was she kidding?

Michael was sitting out on the grass beneath this big oak tree behind the gym. Normally, he's part of a crowd, but he was by himself, his back against the tree, long legs stretched out in front. He was twisting a piece of grass between his fingers.

"Hey, Donna. How's things?" He hardly even glanced up.

I sat down next to him, where he couldn't avoid looking at me. "You're not going to believe what she's done now." I tried to get just the right tone – concern for him, but slightly ticked off at her. I held out the note and, after a while, he took it. I allowed myself a smile then, just a little one. "I mean, just who does she think she is?"

Michael didn't say anything, just folded the note up carefully and put it in the back pocket of his jeans.

"We could pass it around, and then a whole bunch of us can turn up at The Coffee House. It would be so funny." I could just see it – Michael and me together – and the amazed look on Anna's face. Me giving his hand a reassuring squeeze every now and then.

When Michael finally spoke his voice was low. "Donna, you're supposed to be Anna's friend. And here you want to set her up, humiliate her. She's been a jerk the last month, for sure. But why do this? You really are vicious!"

I couldn't believe it. He was going to take all this crap from her, pretend this never happened and go on playing Ken to her Barbie! He just didn't get it. "Michael! The point is, you all accept whatever she does. She snaps her fingers and everyone jumps. She's making you look a jerk!"

I thought that would get him, but he just shook his head. "I know that. But she couldn't help herself. Everyone's entitled to make mistakes. At least Anna never means to harm anyone."

I got up and walked away. This wasn't how it was meant to turn out.

I went down to The Coffee House. I watched her for an hour, sipping the coffee I know she hates and trying not to cry. I never told anyone, though. There was no point. After all, gold just keeps on shining. It's only us cheap imitations that tarnish and get junked.

Small-Town Napoleon

Picture this: a kid who works hard at school, gets good grades, is reasonably popular, doesn't hang with a bad crowd, is polite to his elders, helps around the house without protest, can be relied upon to baby-sit his younger brother and sister. Sounds ideal, huh? A kid any parent would want? Well, if you thought that, you haven't met my dad, the redoubtable Dr. Vincent Li. Hey, maybe I'm being too hard on him – there never were any problems till last summer, but then I'd always toed the line before.

I didn't even notice the poster on the arts bulletin board announcing the auditions, but two of my friends, Jon Anspach and Brian Pulowski did, which was kind of surprising.

"Whoa, gotta go out for this, Brian." Jon was winking in an exaggerated way.

Brian pushed up his glasses with his forefinger. "For sure! Can't miss a chance like this."

"A chance like what?" Sometimes it seemed they talked a whole different language from me.

Brian elbowed me in the ribs. "Girls." He smiled at me, waited, then sighed. "They always go to things like this. Guys don't. So-o-o? Don't you get it?"

I got it.

We'd all discovered girls in a big way that year, but we hadn't cracked the code of actually talking to them without sounding like total jerks. Here was a chance to be around them without too much competition, and one girl in particular would be there – Anna Murphy, who's in the grade above us. To say she is a teen goddess doesn't do it. She's every boy's fantasy – blond, tall, pretty, popular – need I go on? She has one flaw; she's totally unaware of our existence, but we were determined to change all that.

Jon looked at us. "Well, what do you think? Shall we give it a try?"

"Nah, she'll never notice. We'll look like real dorks." Even twenty minutes in close proximity to Anna wasn't worth that.

"Oh, come on, Andy, it'll be a laugh." Jon was looking from Brian to me. "We won't even get a part. I mean, it's some sort of musical version of *Animal Farm*. Can you see us singing and dancing?"

I saw it: short chunky Brian, tall thin Jon and me, Mr. Average, high-kicking our way across a stage, chorus-line style. It just cracked me up. The others assumed that my helpless laughter meant that I'd do it.

The whole thing kind of slipped my mind after that. I didn't even bother mentioning it at home, even though my dad has to know just about everything that happens at school. He can be weird about things. Like, I could have got on to some of the school teams – McMahon, the phys ed teacher, was always on my case about that – but I never went out for them because I knew Dad would think they were a waste of time. Only academic stuff counts. It's because of how hard he had to struggle back in Hong Kong just to finish high school, let alone go on to study medicine, but it's a real drag at times. You come home with 98 per cent on a test and he wants to know what happened to the other 2 per cent. Anyway, I wasn't going to get a part, and even if I did, a play might just be all right – it's literature, right?

But anyway, I'd forgotten about the auditions, so it was a surprise when Jon and Brian set off after lunch on Friday, in the direction of the drama studio. I'd never done any drama, so I had no idea what to expect. Noise, that's what hit me – with Miss Grainger and Mrs. Snow shouting to be heard over it; the music teacher playing scales on an old beat-up piano in the corner of the room. It was enough to give you a headache. And the people – I was surprised by how many had turned up. And not just the girls and arty types – even some of the guys on the football team were there, sitting with Michael Rizzo, who used to be Anna's boyfriend. Anna was near the front, and Brian and Jon squirmed their way through the crowd until they found a seat where they could stare at her, like puppies begging for a treat. They had no style.

"Quiet! Quiet!" Mrs. Snow finally managed to shut everybody up. For such a tiny woman, she's got a really loud voice. "We haven't got a lot of time, so if you don't get seen today, come back same time on Monday. If, after the auditions are over, you don't get a part, we still need help with costumes, stage management and lighting."

Jon and Brian brightened up at that. They think they're real scientific whiz kids, and fooling about with lighting is something they'd think was really cool.

Miss Grainger took over then, explaining the drill. It didn't sound too bad – most practices would be in the lunch hour until about a month before the performance. Then there'd be two Sunday dress rehearsals and some sessions after school during the week. Now, all they wanted was to hear us read and sing. I shot Brian and Jon the look of death – by rushing down to the front they'd just about made sure we'd be called up early.

Brian and two girls were picked first. Miss Grainger had him read Squealer, the little pig who spread the propaganda. I could see his book shaking and there were big drops of sweat on his forehead. I was surprised when he started reading, though. He was OK – persuasive and kind of slimy. Then he had to sing. You got a choice of "O Canada" or "Happy Birthday," but it wouldn't have mattered – Brian was bad, a one-note rumble.

I was in the next three called, with Jon and Anna. I had to read Napoleon, the chief pig, and they were Boxer and Clover, the horses. Lucky we'd studied Orwell's book last year, so I had a good idea what Napoleon was supposed to be like. But each step to the stage still felt ten feet high. I'd lost all sensation in my legs, and I had to look down to see where my feet should go. I knew I looked like a jerk and everyone was staring. I stuttered out my first line, fighting this huge rushing sound in my ears, but then suddenly, all I could think about was this pig and how much he despised these horses, who were so stupid and easy to con. Brian said Miss Grainger had to say my name twice to get me to stop.

"Thank you, that was fine. Let's hear you sing now." I started "O Canada" but I couldn't tell you how it sounded. Even when we got back to our seats, I was still feeling strange, like I wasn't really there. I had to struggle to follow what people were saying.

"Hey, you two weren't bad." Brian balanced his chair on two legs. "At least you can both sing."

"What's next? Do we go or stay?" Jon asked.

Brian shook his head. "No idea."

Anna turned around and smiled. She had these really white teeth and a freckle to one side of her mouth, like a blob of chocolate. "The cast list will go up next week. If you're not on it, they'll ask you about working backstage. They're good like that. People think Miss Grainger can be mean, but she's OK once you get to know her."

Boy, was this different. Since the business with that student teacher last year, people said Anna had changed – but being nice about a teacher? Talking to some Grade 11 jerks?

I nodded, muttering, "Thanks," surprised I was able to speak at all. It was just as well I could because the other two had reverted to silent doggy devotion, and it was all they could do to keep their tongues from hanging out.

All I could think about was telling my parents about the auditions and the odd feeling I'd had, about how right it had seemed being up on stage. We do most of our talking at the dinner table – if Dad's not on call, that is. So, I figured I'd wait till then; at least I wouldn't have to go through everything twice. I kind of liked the idea of thinking about it for a while anyway, how good it had felt being someone else, not just Andy Li, all-round Mr. Nice Guy.

Dad arrived home about ten minutes before dinner was ready. I heard the garage door slam. He shouted a greeting and went straight upstairs to wash. Mum turned from the stove and looked at me. "Set the table, Andy, and get Lilian and Robert to wash their hands." During the week, we eat in the kitchen, so it took about ten seconds to put out bowls, chopsticks and serving spoons. I carried the rice cooker over from the counter and put it by Mum's place at the table before I went looking for the kids. They were down the basement watching television but only gave a token argument about having to come and eat.

Dad was already sitting at the table. He had taken off his jacket and rolled up his shirt sleeves but was still wearing a tie. He barely glanced up from his empty bowl as we came in. Mum motioned us to sit down and gave Robert and Lilian the look that said, act up at your own risk! She brought over a platter of *dun goo jing gai*, and another of bok choy with shrimp, which she laid in the centre of the table before serving rice into everyone's bowl. I waited. This was the time Dad normally interrogated the three of us about school, but he remained silent, gloomily jabbing at a piece of chicken. His fingers were clenched so tightly that they had ivory-coloured blotches matching the chopsticks. He lifted his head and spoke, a quick rush of Cantonese. Lilian and Robert looked confused – their Cantonese is not very good, but it was all I spoke till I started school here, so I was able to understand what was wrong.

"I just can't understand it, Margaret. I sponsor my mother to come from Hong Kong. I do all the paperwork, make all the arrangements. Now she'd rather live in Toronto with Ray than with us!"

Dad takes his role as eldest son very seriously, especially now that his father is dead. He and my uncle are always at each other about this. It's complicated, but Ray is the only one of his brothers and sisters that Dad didn't put through university. It's not like he didn't offer, but Ray wanted to go his own way. It doesn't help that Ray's the only one in the family with any real money, all made from his electronics company. It's some power struggle.

Mum reached and lifted a piece of bok choy into Lilian's bowl. "I don't think she means it to hurt you, Vincent. But

Toronto's probably best for her. She doesn't speak much English, and apart from us and the Chus, who is there in Elmwood for her to talk to? She'd be terribly isolated. In Toronto, she's got a whole Chinese community – several, in fact – and she'll be able to see all your brothers and sisters far more easily. You sponsored her to be with the family, after all."

Dad sighed. "You're right." He ran his hand through his hair. "It was the way I was told – a phone call from Ray rather than from her. I could tell he was smirking."

Mum laughed. "Vincent, that's going a bit far. You and your brother may not get on, but he doesn't set out deliberately to hurt you."

We all sat there, watching Dad. The two little kids might not have understood what was being said exactly, but they knew that with Dad it could go one of two ways – either he would laugh and calm down or he would go into one of his mega temper tantrums, shouting in Cantonese and slamming around the house. Mum's used to it, just ignores him till he's through, but it's scary for the rest of us.

We were lucky that night. Robert had been holding a piece of chicken over his bowl and it suddenly fell, sliding across the polished table. Dad laughed and shouted, "Oho, chopstick failure!" Everyone relaxed, and no more was said about my grandmother. Still, I didn't think this was the time to tell them about the audition. Maybe I'd tell Mum later and let her tell Dad.

The rest of the evening just slipped away. Whenever we've avoided one of Dad's blow-outs, we tread kind of carefully. He either acts like nothing happened or he's super jolly, wanting to take us out for dinner or planning some kind of treat. Either way, anything, something really stupid, could set him off again. Lilian and Robert didn't protest when Mum sent them to their rooms early to play awhile before bed. From my room I could hear them, but only muffled thumps and giggles. I got stuck into my homework, letting math problems block everything else out. I heard the phone and then Dad going out, so I slipped downstairs to talk to Mum. She was sitting on the leather sofa, her feet curled under her, deep in some Chinese film that one of my aunts had lent her last time we were in Toronto. I could see tears trickling down her face as she stared at the screen, and she wiped them away with the back of her hand. I watched her for a few seconds and crept quietly back up to my room.

Brian, Jon and I didn't talk much about the play. It seemed kind of pointless. Jon and Brian thought they'd probably help with the lights, but I wasn't sure that I wanted to. So, it was a bit of a surprise when a week later Anna Murphy came running towards me.

"Andy, congratulations! I knew you'd get it."

To be approached by your dream girl is shocking enough, but when she even knows your name it leaves you speechless. All I managed was "Wha . . . ?"

"The play. They've cast you as Napoleon." Her face showed she was discovering that I was a total moron and wondering why she was wasting her time.

I just took off running – whatever else she said was lost as I headed for the arts bulletin board.

Anna was right. OK, it was dumb to doubt her but, hey, I wasn't thinking straight. In bold black type that seemed to vibrate as I stared at it:

Napoleon - Andrew Li

It was like someone had punched me in the stomach – I actually stopped breathing. It was maybe even minutes before I made sense of the rest. Anna was in, too, playing Clover – I hadn't even asked her if she'd got a part. Brian was part of the pigs' chorus and Squealer's understudy. Jon wasn't there at all.

People were knocking into me as they made their way to the first class of the afternoon, but I couldn't move. This just felt so right, like some part of me had been missing and now I'd found it. The only problem was going to be at home.

When I got there Robert had his brat face on, eyeing his slice of cake and Lilian's. "She's got more than I have!"

"No, I haven't, and even if I have, so what! I'm bigger than you." Lilian had curved her arm around her plate, daring Robert to make a grab for it.

Leaning against the counter, Mum watched them. I stood beside her, dumping my backpack on the floor by the table.

"Andy, why do these two always argue? What do they want me to do – measure each slice with a ruler?" She smiled and patted my arm. "At least I have one sensible kid now. Did you have a good day?"

"Yeah, I . . ." Would it be better to wait, tell Dad at the same time? Nah, it was too late. The words were already coming out and I knew I had this huge stupid grin on my face. "I tried out for the school play and . . ." My smile was getting bigger, so that it felt like my face would split. "And I heard today that I made it. I got a part, Mum!"

She smiled back at me, looking a little puzzled. "That's wonderful, I think. But you've never done anything like this before."

"I know, but that's what's so weird. I only went because Jon and Brian wanted to go, but once I got up on that stage it was like something that had been waiting for me all my life. I can't explain it, really." I shook my head and glanced sideways at her. "What do you think, eh? My son, the actor!"

Mum laughed. "It'll certainly be a first in this family. Well, why not? What's the play?"

"*Animal Farm*, a musical version. I'm Napoleon." This didn't mean a thing to Mum, but it felt great just saying it out loud.

Lilian stopped chewing and cocked her head, a fat bunch of hair threatening to end up in the mess on her plate. "I've seen that at school. It's a cartoon." She snorted with laughter. "Napoleon's a big fat pig!"

Half-chewed cake sprayed out of Robert's mouth onto the table and he started to chant, "Andy is a pi-ig! Andy is a pi-ig!"

I picked up a magazine from the counter and took a pretend swat at him. That was all he needed to be up and running around the table as he chanted. I wrestled him to the floor, tickling until he couldn't stop giggling.

Still sitting on the floor, I looked up at Mum. "What do you think Dad will say?"

She spread her hands. "Andy, you know what he's like." She walked over to the table and picked up the plates, sweeping crumbs from the table onto one of them. "If you put it the right way, who knows?"

I felt a deadness spread through me. I knew I'd have to persuade Dad, but I hadn't thought about not being able to do the play. Mum's noncommittal answer scared me.

"Look, Andy, he's going to be late tonight. Why don't you wait and eat with us?" She nodded in the direction of Robert and Lilian. "I'll feed certain other persons early so that they'll be in bed by then. You won't have any distractions." She gave Robert a poke as he started to whisper, "Pi-ig, pi-ig!"

I went to my room to start my homework but looked out the window every time I heard a car. It was so stupid. In my head I rehearsed everything, playing up how this would help with my English (Dad wouldn't remember we studied *Animal Farm* in Grade 10), how it would look good on my college application – you know, the "well-rounded" person and all that crap – and how I wouldn't let it affect my other subjects. I was so convincing that there was no way anyone could refuse me, especially not with my best good-boy smile, modest but sincere.

Maybe I got overconfident, but all I know is I didn't read the signs when Dad finally got home around eight-thirty. As soon as I heard his voice, I was on my way down, taking the stairs two at a time. He was in the kitchen by then, his back to me as he washed his hands at the sink before sitting down at the table.

"Andrew." A nod acknowledging my presence, nothing more. He just sat there staring down at his bowl, not even glancing up when Mum brought over the tureen of tofu soup.

My stomach was twisting itself in knots. I could feel my pulse quicken. "Dad?" I stopped, catching Mum's quick shake of the head, but it was too late. I had to know, get my answer. "I auditioned for the school play a couple of weeks back."

That got his attention. He looked straight at me for the first time.

"I got a part, just about the lead – Napoleon in *Animal Farm*." My voice sounded so calm, almost flat, hiding how much this meant to me.

Dad's face was blank.

Yes! I thought. It's going to be OK.

"You'll have to tell them you can't do it." Dad picked up a spoonful of soup, started blowing on it. His voice was calm. He didn't look at me or Mum.

It felt like he'd hit me. I wasn't breathing. All I could do was stare, as he drank his soup, and then look from him to Mum, who avoided my eyes.

"Why? It's an honour. I tried out against a whole lot of others for the part. *Animal Farm* is one of our required books." I sounded whiny and desperate, all my polished arguments forgotten.

Dad looked up. "Andrew, I said no. It will take too much time – your schoolwork will suffer."

My heart was really thudding now. "It won't, I promise. Dad, please, I've got to do it." All the time I talked his face was stiffening, but I didn't care. He had to realize how important this was to me. "My grades won't slip. If they do, I'll drop out of the play. Come on, Dad. You're not being fair. I always do what you and Mum want – work hard at school, baby-sit Lilian and Robert. I really want this. It's something I could be good at . . ."

My voice died away as I watched his rage form and fight its way out in a flood of Cantonese directed straight at me.

"Now, you just listen to me. This acting is for people who don't want to go anywhere. When I was your age I studied, I studied under the pillow, I studied all day. I read books, books and books. And you just go and do the same! We are not rich people. We are not like those people who drive a big Mercedes. We started off very poor. We used to live in two rooms smaller than this, and that was for the whole family. Huh? You understand?"

He pushed back his chair and paced around the table, still shouting, waving his hand to indicate the room. "We've done all this to send you to school. And you, you want to go acting?"

What was so bad? Why he was taking this like a personal attack?

He caught something on my face, "You, hey, you! You just listen to me. You listen good. You don't study, you end up in the streets. Where is it written in this whole wide world that you don't study, you get anywhere? Where? Where? You show me. You show me."

He paused for breath and turned, bending down so his face was right in mine. "You're going from bad to worse. You're a bad son! You don't listen to me. You don't listen to your elders. You are going to get nowhere, nowhere. The problem with you – I know it, I know it – is that you've been reading too many of those barbarian books. We should have sent you to good Chinese school, learn some Chinese values."

When it showed no sign of stopping, Mum caught my eye and, with a quick jerk of her head, indicated that I should leave.

Dad followed me to the door, still shouting, jabbing the

air as he listed all my failings. I felt an anger as fierce as his start inside me.

In my room, I sat on the floor, my hands flat on the carpet, my head on my knees, listening to the argument downstairs. Mum put up a good fight – her soothing voice kept working away, but my father just got louder and louder. The door opened and I was suddenly sandwiched between Lilian's and Robert's tense, wiry bodies. They were crying.

"Hey, guys, it's OK." I put my arms around them and pulled them close. "It's nothing to do with you." We stayed like that until the study door slammed and the stereo came on, blasting out Beethoven. Lilian and Robert stayed pressed against me, but I felt their bodies relax and their breathing slow down. There was no protest when I led them back to their rooms and tucked them into bed.

In my own room, I fingered the shiny covers of *Animal Farm*, tracing the outlines of the pig dominating the farmyard.

My head felt packed with wet cotton balls when Lilian and Robert came running in the next morning, all their fright gone, and launched themselves onto my bed.

"Hey, what happened to knocking?"

Both of them grinned, and Lilian, her knees on either side of my chest, leaned forward until her nose touched mine. I could smell milk and cereal on her breath, and she had several Rice Crispies stuck like a comic moustache above her mouth. "Guess where we're all going this Saturday?"

Robert bounced up and down, "Yeah, guess!"

We only ever went one place as a family on the weekends, but they were getting a kick out of this, "Er, Moosonee . . . Medicine Hat . . . the moon!"

As each guess got dumber, they giggled. Unfortunately, they also jumped on me and their knees were sharp. So I wasn't exactly heart-broken when Robert burst out as if it were some huge surprise, "Toronto! We're going for dim sum with the family and then to Uncle Ray's. It'll be neat. Mark's got a new video game me and him can play."

"And me!" Lilian looked dangerously at him,

"Yeah, well, I'm sure you two will sort it out. How about letting me up so I can get dressed."

A few token bounces later I was free, and as I washed and dressed, all the gloom of the previous night came back. There was no way I was going to let it drop. I didn't care how many times Dad lost his temper, he had to let me try this. I was going to be calm, though, just tell him straight.

Walking into the kitchen slowly, I took a deep breath, but only Mum was there. She waved me towards the round pine table where she had set out juice, cereal and milk. "Gone to work already," she said in answer to my look. Her skin was a pale olive in the bright sunshine, and she looked tired. "You've heard we're going to Toronto on the weekend?"

"Yeah." I kept my head down, pretending to concentrate on pouring milk in my bowl.

Sighing, Mum came and sat across from me, her hands around a mug of coffee. "Your uncle called yesterday afternoon to invite us. He wants to talk to your dad about Ben. Ben's decided he wants to go to medical school, so they want some advice about which universities offer the best courses." She gave me a weak smile.

Dad was always bugging me to fast-track, concentrate

on the sciences so I could get into medical school, like it was a foregone conclusion that I wanted to be a doctor. But I had no idea what I wanted to do, so I always fought to take as a wide a variety of subjects as I could. It must have really irked him that Ben, Ray's eldest son, wanted to do just what Dad's always pushing at me. Toss in my announcement about the play and home run for Uncle Ray, strike three for Dad.

"Yeah, well . . . it's not right, losing his temper like that. He won't even listen." My spoon was trailing through the cereal in my bowl.

"I know, Andy, but he does try. He used to blow up far more often. You were probably too little to remember what it was like when we first came to Canada, when he was working so hard to become established in Elmwood, to get his brothers and sisters over as well. It was really tough. We were the only Chinese family in town, but this was the only place he could find a practice that looked as if it might lead somewhere." Mum's eyes were begging me to understand.

So what if he was better now. It still wasn't fair.

"There's so much about your father you'll never understand – all that 'Chinese stuff,' as Robert calls it."

"If it makes him act like a lunatic, maybe I don't want to understand." Looking up, I asked, "Did you talk to him this morning? Has he calmed down? I can do the part, can't I?"

Taking one of my hands, Mum sighed again. "I tried, Andy. You shouldn't have pressed him so hard last night. He's backed into a corner now, where he feels that if he goes back on what he said, he'll lose face."

My glass of orange juice nearly went over as I jerked my hand angrily away. "I can't do something that means so much to me because he's so stiff-necked he can't admit he was wrong? You expect me to accept that?"

"Andy, calm down. If you let it drop now, do what he wants, I can work on him. When the next play comes around, he'll probably see things differently."

"Oh, yeah, Mum, sure. Like they'll automatically offer me the lead again, just like that." She winced as I stamped out of the kitchen.

It was already hot when I hit the pavement running. I didn't want to see anyone so I took the long way around, avoiding Edna's Variety, where I normally hooked up with my friends. It's not fair! pounded in my brain in the rhythm of my feet hitting the sidewalk.

The morning passed. I made the right noises, did the usual things, but I felt like I was covered in bubble wrap, muffled from everything around me. At the first rehearsal I'd have to tell them I couldn't do it. Either that or make life hell at home.

I tried to find Miss Grainger or Mrs. Snow between classes, but no luck. I thought if I went to the rehearsal early, maybe I'd get a chance to talk to them alone. It was amazing, though – half the cast was already in the drama studio when I turned up ten minutes early. There was no sign of Miss Grainger or Mrs. Snow, but I saw a hand down front wave in my direction. Anna was sitting there with a group of people from her grade.

"This is Andy Li. He's the one who blew them all away at the audition. He's going to be Napoleon."

Blushing, I mumbled something and was almost relieved when I saw Mrs. Snow come through the door. I made straight for her, but before I could speak, she dumped a load of books in my arms, telling me to give them out. By the time I'd done that, Miss Grainger had turned up and they got right down to it.

I'd thought we'd start off reading through the play until we knew our parts and then we'd work on the movements or something. But they began with this being an ensemble piece, whatever that meant, and how we had to work together as a group, so we'd start off by getting used to one another. We did these "trust" exercises. In one, we all stood in a small, tight circle. The person in the middle had to close their eyes and then let themselves fall towards the circle, where the others caught them and then pushed them off in another direction to be caught again. It was weird when you were the one in the middle, sort of scary but relaxed at the same time. Everyone was quiet, like in church or something, and all you could hear was people breathing and the tick of the clock. It began to get a little tense, so it was almost a relief when Brian was the middle guy. He's not fat exactly, just sort of solid, and when he fell towards Mrs. Snow, she actually staggered back and the people next to her had to help her hold him up and push him away. He was great, though, didn't even open his eyes once, just kept this really dumb grin on his face. Soon we were all laughing, pretending not to be able to hold him when he came towards us.

If this was what they did in all drama courses, I'd really missed out, but Dad had always sniffed, saying drama was a "peripheral subject." We finished up by pairing off and finding out all we could about our partner in a minute and then introducing them to the group. After that, Miss Grainger and

Mrs. Snow just swept out of the room before I'd had a chance to talk to them. It kind of seemed like fate then.

The only bad time was when I went home that afternoon. I kicked off my shoes in the mud room and then headed into the kitchen. Instead of Mum and the kids, Dad was sitting at the table reading the grocery flyer. It was so weird. I held my breath, but he barely glanced up at me.

"Good day at school, Andrew?"

"Yeah, OK." Expecting more, I shifted from foot to foot. He was back into the flyer, reading it like it was the most fascinating thing he had ever seen. Typical. Act like everything was fine and maybe it would be.

My mother was going to be more difficult. After my temper tantrum that morning, running out on her the way I did, she wasn't going to let me off the hook so easily. There was no sign of her downstairs, so I thought I would hang out in my room till she found me. That came sooner than I figured. As I rounded the bend in the stairs, there was Mum, balanced on a step-ladder, trying to wrestle a suitcase down through the narrow opening to the attic. Another suitcase, coated with dust, lay on the carpet at the bottom of the ladder.

"Oh, Andy, there you are. Give me a hand and take these two into the bedroom."

All sorts of things whirled around in my head. They must have shown because Mum managed a shaky smile. "Don't look so worried. It's bad but not that bad. My father called from Hong Kong this morning. Ah-por's worse. She's not expected to get better and she wants to see all her children." Mum was talking as she followed me into her bedroom. "I've managed to get on a flight tomorrow, so we'll need you to pick up Lilian and Robert from school and look after them until your dad gets back from the airport."

Relief rushed through me. Then I felt bad because she was too preoccupied with my grandmother's illness to think about the play. "How long will you be gone?" That sounded selfish and whiny. Mum hardly ever got to see her family and now she was only getting to go back because Ah-por was dying.

Mum had opened the closet doors and started pulling out skirts and dresses, which she laid on the bed. "I don't know, Andy. It could be a week or it could be a month. The doctors can't say exactly how long she'll last, and then I'll have to stay for the funeral. If I don't, everyone will talk and my father will be shamed."

I hated the way her voice sounded so flat and tired. "What about us?" I'd done it again. "Dad can't cope on his own."

"No, but we've spent the day sorting things out. Your father's mother arrives next week. She'll come here and help out, but it's not going to be easy." Mum was wrapping pairs of shoes in old plastic bags, putting them in a careful border inside the suitcase. She straightened up and looked at me. "A lot of responsibility will fall to you, Andy. She's new to the country and speaks almost no English. You'll have to do the marketing for her as well as helping her with Robert and Lilian because they speak so little Cantonese. Will you do that?"

"No problem." I sounded more confident than I felt. Since we came to Canada I'd only seen Dad's mother twice, but she really scared me, all quick-fire bursts of Cantonese, poking fingers and definite ideas about everything. "I'll get the kids to help with the housekeeping."

"I knew I could rely on you, Andy. Don't worry about the cleaning. Miss Brunowski who cleans your father's office is going to come every day to do that. Try not to aggravate your dad, OK? He's going to be under a lot of stress."

That made me remember how mad I was at Dad, the way we have to tiptoe around him like he's some sort of bomb about to go off. "Don't worry, I'll be a good little boy." I knew it sounded sullen.

"Don't put yourself down." Mum looked at her watch. "Can you go find Robert and Lilian? Dad's going to take you to Chu's restaurant while I finish my packing."

"Sure." I tried not to smile, but all my problems seemed to have vanished. So, why did I feel like a creep?

Mum's mother took more than two months to die. We got used to the phone calls from Hong Kong, the funny letters Mum found time to write us even when she was spending most of her time at the hospital. Things were OK at home. Dad was around more but on his best behaviour. We had his mother to thank for that.

Ah-ma, as we called her, was hardly taller than Lilian and probably weighed no more than eighty pounds, but you'd have to be crazy to take her on. All flashing eyes and sharp commands, she had us all toeing the line in no time. Even Dad. It must have been tough, not understanding much English, alone in the house all day except when Miss Brunowski came in to clean. Every day when I got home from school, I got the feeling that she was waiting for me, needing someone who could talk to her.

One day, a week or so before Mum came back, I was late.

Mrs. Snow had started some after-school rehearsals — just for the leads. I swear Ah-ma must have been waiting by the door — it jerked open as I reached for the doorknob.

"Ah Chu." My grandmother was the only person who ever used my Chinese name, which was probably just as well. "At last you're here. I've been waiting. Ah Sek wants something, but I'm not sure what. He tried to show me but I didn't understand. He went to the phone, I think to call your father, but I wouldn't let him. I told him your father is busy and must not be disturbed."

Robert hated not getting his own way and could make a huge fuss. When he finally got to Dad, my lateness would need some explanation. I patted Ah-ma's hand. "Don't worry. I'll try and sort it out."

The television was on in the basement and there was Robert, sprawled on the sofa, tear tracks on his flushed cheeks. "Andy!" He threw his arms around my waist. "She wouldn't let me. Not even when I explained."

"Hey, slow down. Let you what?"

It all came out in a muddled rush. "Go with Zach. To the arena. His brother's playing and his mum said she'd take us all for pizza after. She wouldn't even let me call Dad, and you weren't home." Tears were starting to edge out again. "I hate her! She's mean. I wish Mum was back."

I pushed him back, keeping my hands on his shoulders. "Hey, Robbo, Ah-ma's not being mean. She just didn't understand, that's all. Look, is it too late to go now? It's just six." I was desperate to settle this.

Robert sniffed a few times. "The game starts at six-thirty, but they were going to go early because Zach's brother had to practise."

"No problem." I sighed with relief as his face brightened. "I'll call them and if they've already left, we'll go straight to the arena, OK?" From Robert's rush to get up the basement stairs, I guessed it was.

When I got back, Ah-ma was in the kitchen chopping garlic and ginger. She had Lilian at the table shredding spring onions. "Ah Sek is happy?" she asked.

"Yes. He's with his friend now and his friend's mother will bring him back after supper."

Lilian sniffed, having guessed that we were talking about Robert. "He's such a baby, crying just because he can't go to some stupid old hockey game."

Ah-ma handed Lilian some mushrooms to slice. "I was worried, Ah Chu. He was so angry and upset, and you were late." She looked sideways at me.

"Oh, I stayed to work on a science project with my friends. We needed to use the lab. This is the only time it was free, and the teacher was willing to stay after school." I was glad that I was speaking Cantonese because I was pretty sure that Lilian would have caught me out in English.

Sitting next to Lilian, Ah-ma smoothed the top of her *sam-fu* over the matching trousers. "You're just like your father."

A bubble of laughter lodged in my throat and I nearly choked, forcing it down. Like Dad?

"He always worked so hard, too. It was difficult for him, sharing a room with all his brothers. He used to spend his time at the library — it was the only quiet place where he could work. And when he came home after it shut" — she laughed at the memory — "he used to work by flashlight while his brothers slept. You remind me of him so much, Ah Chu."

This time I couldn't help it. I did laugh.

"No. No, you do," Ah-ma went on. "You look after the little ones like he did with his brothers and sisters."

"Can't you guys talk English — all this is boring, OK?" Lilian's voice cut across Ah-ma's. "Ask if these mushrooms are sliced thin enough, Andy?"

I'd never done anything that I loved so much as that play. The others probably thought I was a real jerk — everything was fun for me: learning my lines, watching when I wasn't on stage, making the papier-mâché animal masks, even the singing, which I thought would be a real embarrassment. When some of the kids complained about the extra rehearsals, Mrs. Snow told them that her idea of heaven was endlessly rehearsing Chekhov. I wasn't too sure who Chekhov was — until I looked him up I thought he was that character in the old *Star Trek* — but I knew what she meant. It was like I'd come home.

With Mrs. Snow's help, I started to check out some of the universities where you could take drama. Since she hadn't fallen down laughing when I first asked her about it, I guess she thought I might have a chance, but she kept telling us how hard it was to make it as an actor and that's why she'd ended up teaching.

I was so happy that I wanted to tell them at home all about it. I'd never lied big time before. I mean I've told a few little lies but nothing major like this — this was a whole other life. I tried to tell myself I wasn't actually lying, just not telling, that's all. Dad didn't make it any easier, suddenly becoming Mr. Nice Guy.

A couple of times, on weekends, he came with me when I did the shopping and then would suggest that we stop and have a coffee. It was weird. Here was this guy who only ever used to talk to me about school or tell me what to do, really opening up – about himself and about Mum being away.

"Your grandmother tells me you've been asking about what it was like when I was growing up." Dad stirred his coffee, not looking at me.

"Yeah, well. You don't talk about it much and I was curious, that's all. No big deal." It sounded like he thought I'd been prying.

"A bit different, eh?" His smile was quick, leaving his face with its usual guarded expression.

"I never thought about how small Granddad's apartment was. I didn't know you shared it with another family. Four of you shared one room?"

"A room smaller than the one you have all to yourself."

"Why didn't you move to some bigger place?"

Dad laughed, "You've been spoiled in Canada. Hong Kong's very crowded, and that was all he could afford. It got easier once I moved out and was working." Dad smiled again, this time a gentle smile that stayed. "It's a great credit to your mother that she married me, knowing how tough it was going to be. With all my younger brothers and sisters, it was up to me to pay for their education if they didn't win scholarships. My father barely made enough money to house and feed them. Once you were born, money was even tighter. That's the main reason we came here."

The waitress arrived with our bill and, as he fished in his pocket for his wallet, Dad spoke again, his voice softer. "I know you think I'm hard on you about school, Andy, but for people like us it is the key, the only way out. I want you to make the most of all the opportunities you have."

People like us? The way out? Didn't he realize it was different here?

A week before the play, Mum arrived home, looking tired and smaller than I remembered. She flinched at the noise that seem to fill our house, and it took her a while to get used to things again, which was just fine by me.

"Andy, where are you going? It's my first weekend back. I was hoping the whole family could spend the day together." I was trying to sneak through the laundry room but Mum was there.

It was the Sunday of our final dress rehearsal. "Jon's. We're working on a science project."

Mum looked up from the pile of clothing she was folding, "From what your Ah-ma says, this must be some project. She's hardly seen you this past week."

I looked away. "Yeah, I know. I feel bad about it, but she said she could cope. The project's due at the end of the week and we goofed up a couple of experiments. That's what slowed us down."

Mum sighed. "Well, you'd better go, then. What time will you be back?"

"About six. I'll call if I'm going to be later." I turned quickly so that she couldn't see my face. I hated lying to her.

We went through the play without stopping. Miss Grainger prompted a couple of times, but that was all. At the end when all the pigs and men stare out at the audience, it was so weird. There was complete silence, and then Jon and the two guys from Grade 12 who did the lights started clapping and the sound echoed around the darkened hall. I had this funny feeling at the back of my neck, like the hairs there were standing up. That was the good part. The bad came when the lights went up and Mrs. Snow had four pages of notes on the run-through. For me, she wanted me to sound more drunk and arrogant when I sang my solo.

That night was one of the best ever. I was excited and scared at the same time. It was all I could do not to tell everyone at dinner. Mum had put a lot of effort into the meal; with Ah-ma's help she had created a real banquet. Everyone's favourite dish: hot-and-sour soup for me, duck with taro for Lilian, spare ribs in the sticky black sauce Robert loved, *tung choy* with dried shrimp sauce for Dad. It was like Christmas and Chinese New Year all rolled in one. Robert and Lilian were on their best behaviour; they didn't argue even once. Dad was cracking jokes like a madman, and kept touching Mum's arm like he wanted to make sure she was really there.

The good feeling lasted all through Monday. The fictitious science project was going to get me out of the house for the two nights of the performance, no problem. It was all taken care of, and I didn't even catch on that something was wrong when I came in after school and found both Mum and Dad at the kitchen table, obviously waiting.

I wasn't even through the door before Dad began speaking. His voice was clipped, each word distinct. "Mrs. Snow called my office today."

I waited for the explosion, but was hurt even more by my mother's soft "Oh, Andy. How could you lie to your father like this?"

"I didn't. Neither of you ever asked whether I'd dropped out." I couldn't look at her. I was staring at my father, who was slowly standing up, pushing his chair carefully away from the table.

When he spoke, his even tone and rigid face scared me. "She very kindly wanted to make sure that we all had our tickets for tonight. Knowing that your mother had been away, she was worried that we might have been too busy to pick them up. So she's left four tickets at the door for us."

For a moment no one spoke. A vein in my father's neck was pulsing like a thick blue snake. His rage, when it came, was almost a relief.

He strode round the kitchen, shouting, hitting out at any object he came close to. The bear cookie jar was swept off the counter and shattered on the floor, crumbs and pieces of china crunching under his feet. He circled me, lashing out with words. I was a liar and an unfit son. I had made him look foolish. I would never amount to anything. I was too soft, too taken with frivolity.

I let his words batter me until he drew in a ragged breath. Then I answered. I didn't scream. I spoke quietly. With my mother's restraining hand on his arm, he listened.

"I didn't want to. I hated it, having to deceive you, but you left me no choice. I had to do this play. I just *had* to. Don't you see, this is *my key*, Dad."

Stopping his rampage round the kitchen, he turned to me, staring. His face was white.

"It's my way out," I said. "I am going tonight and tomorrow night, and I am going to be Napoleon, a pig who thinks he can control everyone and everything."

Tears had started and my nose needed blowing. I half turned to run from the kitchen and through my blurred vision saw Dad moving towards me.

I went to Jon's. He knew something was up, but when I shook my head, he didn't ask. His mother insisted we eat something, but I couldn't swallow. I felt sick, and my father's words kept choking me. After the meal, we sat in silence, the television making conversation. Finally, Jon jumped to his feet, jangling his car keys. "Let's get out of here, Andy. It's early, but you can get costumed up, and there's plenty for me to do. You're making me nervous."

It was easy to get lost in the chaos at school. Miss Grainger grabbed me for make-up as soon as we arrived. The thick pink pancake that would be revealed at the end when my pig mask came off felt slimy and cold.

"Andy, you were just fine Sunday. All you've got to do is turn in that performance again, OK?"

I didn't say anything, just nodded.

She stopped, damp sponge in hand. "Andy, are you all right?" She patted my shoulder. "If you're feeling nervous, don't worry, it's normal. People who've been acting for years still throw up every time they have to perform."

I managed a half-hearted smile.

Reassured, she continued. "It's hard when it's your first time, but you're going to do well. Your parents will be really proud of you."

I had to turn away then, look down so she couldn't see the tears that were threatening again.

"OK, you're done. Go get your costume for the opening."

In the holding area at the back of the stage, people weren't really talking – they were just making comments to hide their nerves, not expecting a reply, and not listening if there was one. I found a corner and sank down into it. The move my father had made towards me was being endlessly replayed in my head. Was he going to hit me? Hold me back? What happened after I left? I pictured Mum listening to him rant. I could see her talking, but couldn't hear what she was saying.

"Guys, this is it!" Mrs. Snow called excitedly, as she cut through the noise.

My head ached as we took our positions on the blacked-out stage. There was a light touch on my hand. Anna whispered, "You're going to be great."

Swung along in blur of colour and sound, my first line came and went, rasped out from a throat that felt like it was lined with sandpaper. But by the time I got to my first song, nothing mattered except defeating Snowball, my rival, and gaining control.

For me, there was no audience until the final scene. Our animal masks removed, we had to stand still and stare out at them, leaving them to wonder which were pigs and which were men. Silence surrounded us, and then the clapping and cheering started. I willed myself just to stare straight ahead.

"Andy! Andy! That's my brother, Andy! The boss of the pigs." Robert's shrill voice led my eyes to the front row.

They were all there, in the seats nearest the centre aisle. Lilian and Robert were jumping up and down. Mum was clapping with her hands above her head. My father stood, matching my stance and stare.

In the dressing room, people were so excited that the

noise seemed to fill every space, even the one in my head. I smiled when people congratulated me, but my face felt stiff, like I still had my mask on. Words came out but they sounded far away, tinny.

Eventually, I made it out into the corridor where friends and parents were waiting. Lilian nearly knocked me off my feet as she rushed up, wanting to know if she could try my mask on. I risked a quick glance over her bobbing head, but only Mum was there.

Her smile was gentle. "Your father's taken Robert to the car, Andy. We'll go pick up Ah-ma at home and then he wants to take us out to the Chu Dynasty for dinner."

I was breathing heavily, fighting the buzzing in my head. I kept seeing him in the kitchen moving towards me.

Mum's hand reached up and brushed a smudge of make-up on my cheek. "He's trying, Andy. Don't be too hard on him."

I still couldn't speak but I saw Dad, my age, bent over his books, struggling to read and write by flashlight while his brothers slept. I linked my arm through Mum's, grabbed Lilian's hand and the three of us walked through the dark alleyway leading to the parking lot, where the lights of the cars shone.

Alternative
Measures

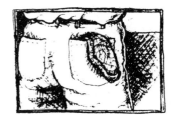

I saw her this morning. First time since school started. Walking down the corridor. There she was – alone, like always. I gave a half-assed wave, muttered, "Hi." She stopped dead, looked at me with those big eyes. People were starting to stare, snicker, looking from her to me. Her back straightened and her chin lifted and she swept on by. Strange feeling. Maybe I was expecting something else. Don't know what, though. Been thinking about her a lot. Don't know why.

Not much makes sense since I came to Elmwood. Everything's mixed up. Things keep changing on me. For a while there was always someone on my back, telling me what to do, driving me crazy. Like Toronto after Gran had to go into the nursing home. That stuck-up jerk Jenni always griping to Dad about me. Worse after she moved in. Didn't like the way I dressed, who I hung with, what I did, what I didn't do. Didn't even like the way I looked at her – she should be so lucky. When she and Dad came home that night, found my friends at the apartment, she was the one that did the yelling.

"How dare you? Look at the mess. Get the hell out!"

Dad stood in the doorway, saying nothing. Face blank.

She charged in, yanked the sound system's plug, screamed till everyone left. Tried to grab me, pushed her face – all white except for these two red dots on her cheeks – close to mine. Shook her off, ran out into the night, found my friends.

When I sneaked back in early next morning, she was still going strong. I could hear her yattering on in their bedroom. Hardly heard Dad, but he got his say next day: I was going to Elmwood to live with Mom. Never asked me what I wanted, just told me. Mom, she had dumped me on Gran and Dad when I was two, gone off bumming around the States. She suddenly want me now? OK, since I was ten she's been in touch, sent me oddball presents, like the silver bracelet she'd made, braided like a biker's leather wristband. She'd even visited me a couple of times, but I'd never been to see her. Well, hey, at least I wouldn't have to put up with Jenni the Jerk.

Mom was OK at first. Tiptoed around me, saying she didn't know how to treat me. She was cool. Until she got the studio at the new art centre, all her jewellery-making stuff was in the living room, so she never bugged me about my mess. Maybe artists are more laid-back.

Anyway, she didn't hassle me, but it was so dull. Elmwood is the armpit of the universe. There's no where to go without a car, nothing to do. Kids here think they're cool if they stay out after eight o'clock. I really missed Queen West, Jake and Tommaso and me, the clubs letting us in even though we were underage. Called a couple of times but it didn't work. They were talking about people I didn't know, gigs they'd been to by bands I'd never heard of. What could I tell them — that the Lions had organized a pancake breakfast?

School was a laugh, though. I loved the looks on those geeks' faces when I mouthed off. It was act out or die of boredom. But teachers are the same everywhere.

"Bob! Enough of that."

"In Toronto, I'm sure such behaviour would be perfectly acceptable as a way of expressing individuality, Bob, but we're not quite so sophisticated here. We won't tolerate it."

"I'll have to speak with your mother."

When they did, she didn't yell or anything. She was just so damn understanding and sad. "What's wrong, Bob? Why are you behaving like this?"

I'd give her my best stone face, the one I used for Jenni the Joke. What Mom was doing was the same, trying to run my life – only she went for the soft approach. Made me twist up inside.

Then she'd get into all this psychological crap. "Is it that you're angry, Bob? Angry with your dad? With me? Talk to me. Tell me how you feel. We've got to live together, so we've got to sort this out."

It was all a load of garbage. If she really cared she'd never have left me in the first place. She was just scared people would say she couldn't control her own kid. I'd stare at the walls, the floor – anything not to see the way she looked at me.

"You've got to make the best of it. I know you don't want to be here, but give it a chance." Her voice got kind of hoarse then. "Give *me* a chance, OK?"

I gave her my hardest stare.

When she couldn't take it any more, she always got straight on the phone to her friend, C.J. Flaherty. Told him what a bad boy I was. Sometimes I'd listen in on the extension. She'd go into this what-was-she-doing-wrong stuff, telling him how I was completely closed down, what would happen if I blew it here in Elmwood, what was to become of me and all that crap.

C.J.'s a lawyer, Elmwood's own legal eagle. From the day I arrived, he'd listen to Mom for a while, be sympathetic and then he'd start in.

"Lisa, you're too soft on him. That's the whole problem — his gran spoiled him and he does exactly as he pleases." Some lawyer, huh? Like what evidence did he have for this crap? "Set Bob some boundaries. That's the way to show you really care."

C.J. was always over at our house. Whenever Mom left us alone, he'd get on my case.

"What is it with you, Bob? Do you enjoy upsetting your mother?" He had this round red face and it'd get redder the angrier he got. "Come on, give her a break. If she hadn't taken you, what would have happened? Think about it, kid. Your father has had it with you. You're running out of options."

Right about there, I'd leave the room. He was just another one like Jenni who didn't want me around. But when the b.s. went down at the community centre he loved it. Here was his chance: save the kid from the evil clutches of the law and impress Mom no end. Crusading lawyer and all-round sensitive guy.

The day we went to the court in Lexington was the worst. We stood in this big hall, all echoing marble, kids milling around, lawyers with their suits and smug faces, parents looking scared. When Mom went to the john, C.J. kept eyeing me like I was going to bolt. He leaned in towards me. I could smell coffee on his breath, see the reddish hairs in his nostrils.

"Do you realize how lucky you are?"

I worked at sounding bored. "Yeah, lucky! Thanks to you, I've got two hundred hours of dumb community service." I didn't want him thinking I was grateful or anything. I knew what his game was. Hadn't even had to go through a trial. C.J. had filled out a few forms, sweet-talked the Crown prosecutor and shown up here with us. Well, big deal.

I thought he was going to hit me then. Nearly stepped back, but that was too easy. Braced myself instead, my grin daring him to take his best shot. "You're a real piece of work, aren't you!" he sneered. "You might be able to jerk your mother around but not me. You were that close, Bob. Your mother had to work very hard for the Elmwood Community Centre to agree to take you and supervise your community service. Paying for the materials to repair the damage you did there helped, too. Without her, you would never have been dealt with under Alternative Measures." He stepped towards me again, running his hand through his gingery hair. "I wouldn't have gone to all that trouble for you. Maybe going through the system would have knocked some sense into you." He shook his head. "I went to the community centre. I saw what you did."

Couldn't help it but I smiled. Back then I thought it was pretty cool – Day-Glo orange and green four-letter words all over the walls where their stupid drop-in club meets. I'd shown them. Let them know I didn't give a damn about getting kicked out.

"I don't believe this. You stand there smirking, feeling hard done by when you've been inches away from going to trial!" People turned around, staring at us. He sighed, half turned away. "I wish I could take you downstairs, show you the holding pen, four or five kids to a cell, like animals in cages."

That did get to me. Not what he said – what I'd seen.

When we were in the court room, they brought this kid up from the cells. He was younger than me, scrawny looking, maybe fourteen. He shuffled in between cops twice his size. They'd chained his feet. Didn't know they'd do that to a kid.

There'd been a recess called then and we'd all left the court room. Mom and C.J. went off in a huddle with Alec Brennan, the worker from Elmwood Community Centre. I hung back, stayed away, didn't want to hear the whole mess again. A kid had come up to me, wanting to bum a cigarette. Got talking to him. It was scary. He'd only been released from detention for a month and was already up for breaking and entering. He'd laughed at me when I asked him about the chains. "They always do that when you're already in custody and they bring you to court. Ankle shackles are no big deal. When they chain your hands as well, that means you're a real bad guy." He grinned. "I'm working on it."

His face had twisted when he saw my look, but then he'd shrugged. "Nothing like that'll happen to you, not with Mommy and Daddy here." He jerked his head in the direction of Mom and C.J., who were moving our way.

I had started to say, "He's not —" but the kid had swaggered off to a group of kids, giving them high fives, then looking back in my direction and sniggering.

C.J.'s hand landed hard on my shoulder. "You're not even listening to me!"

I stared at his bald spot, tried to tune out his voice.

"What does it take to get through to you? Surely even you can understand this." C.J. tightened his grip. "You've got three months to complete your community service to everyone's satisfaction. If you don't, you're dead meat. They'll haul your ass back to court and then it *is* a trial. I'll be your lawyer but that's all I can do. You will not screw this up! Do you understand?"

"Yeah, Yeah. Lay off." I shrugged his hand off my shoulder just as Mom got back.

"What's going on?" She looked at me like I was the one who'd been doing the shouting.

"Same as always," I said, turning my back on them.

The night before I started at the community centre, C.J. came over. After dinner he and Mom sat down, all serious. Made me stay for The Big Talk. I didn't listen, not after the first few minutes. I made the right noises, though. Back then, I still thought that if I played along maybe they'd let me go to Toronto, visit Dad once I'd done my community service. Only thing that kept me going.

Next day, Mom insisted on driving me to the centre. Wanted to make sure I went. Her voice filled the car – how I had to be polite, not antagonize Brennan. How I had to take responsibility for my actions. I tried to tune her out. Stared at the streets. Sometimes I wish there was somewhere I could go where there are no voices, no sound but my own breathing.

When she let me out of the car, I was so glad to get away that I didn't see them at first. Lounging at the base of the war memorial. Some of the jerks from school.

"Bobby! Oh, Bobbeee, please come out and play?" Mark Lister had moved ahead of the others.

Turning so Mom couldn't see, I gave him the finger and walked towards the double doors at the entrance.

"Aw gee, I forgot. Bobby's been a bad boy. He's got to work." Lister thought he was so funny. That chicken was my number-one fan back when I first came to Elmwood but backed off as soon as things with Buddy Covington started to heat up.

Inside the centre, Alec Brennan kept me waiting outside his office for nearly ten minutes while he talked and joked on the phone. Through the open doors, I could hear the jerks outside, still laughing.

Finally, when he called me in, Brennan looked at me like I was a dog-doo he'd found on the bottom of his shoe. Kept me standing, while he leaned back in his fancy swivel chair.

"You're here on sufferance. Do you understand that?"

I just looked at him.

"I have no use for that bleeding-heart plan Flaherty cooked up, but the board fell for it." He twisted his dorky little pony-tail as he talked. "I'm the one who ends up with all the work, who has to make sure you do things right. Just remember, I get to write the report that goes back to the court, so you'd better not mess me around. Got it?"

"Right." I'd heard this speech hundreds of times before. Imagined what it would be like to sink my fist into his flabby face. Brennan thinks he's got a way with kids, thinks we relate to his pony-tail and coloured shirts, but he's just another middle-aged wienie.

"I'm going to be watching you closely." It was starting to sound like bad dialogue from an old movie. Next he'd be telling me that I was coming into this a boy, but would leave it a man! "Joe, the janitor . . ."

OK, I nearly lost it. Joe the Janitor. Sounded like something out of *Leave it to Beaver*. Who else had we got – Bob the Bad Boy and Alec the Armpit?

"Are you listening?"

"I'm all ears."

"Don't try that smart-alec tone with me!" That did it – "smart alec." I tried to make it sound like a cough, but the laugh got away from me.

"Joe will supply with you all the equipment you need. He'll supervise the actual painting, but I'll be checking up – anytime, all the time. Got that?"

I didn't trust myself to speak without spraying him with laughter. Brennan looked at me strangely as he showed me out of his office.

Joe was a surly old guy with a limp. When Brennan finally left, Joe set off down the corridor, expecting me to follow. In the meeting room, he unlocked the double doors to the store cupboard. The bright sunlight made my orange-and-green handiwork glow like neon. Joe got out a bucket, a long-handled mop and a grungy old sponge, which he tossed to me.

"Today you can wash down the walls." Even before he finished talking, he was turning and heading out of the room.

"Wha-at?" I sounded like a little kid, but this was dumb. "Water won't get that off."

Joe stopped, looked at me. "You think I don't know that? Who do you think spent hours trying to get it off when you first done it? You're gonna repaint the whole room and you're gonna do it properly. And properly starts with washing them walls down."

I had no place to go. Everywhere there was someone after me. At home, it was Mom and C.J. Here, I had Brennan playing the heavy and now this old guy. And those jerks from school hanging around outside.

There was one good thing, though — Elly Kovacs.

I'd nearly finished two walls. Joe had been in once, grunted and nodded, which I took to mean I was doing an OK job. Brennan had been in probably twenty times. Every time there was something. Not enough soap. Too much soap. Drips on the floor. The water needed changing. Kept thinking Toronto, to stop me taking a swing at him.

Anyway, I was up the ladder when I heard steps behind me. Thought it was Brennan, so I kind of accidentally slapped the wall hard with the mop, sending spray flying. Heard a gasp but nothing else. Standing in the dark corridor, looking in, was a girl. She didn't move, so I climbed down off the ladder and swaggered over. Recognized her as I got nearer. Elly Kovacs, this real quiet girl in my class at school.

"What the hell are you staring at?" Liked the way she backed away from me.

Her voice was almost a squeak. "I was just coming to get a drink from the machine." She held out a change purse as if to prove it to me.

"Yeah? Well, how come you're getting one here?" I positioned myself in the doorway, pressing a hand on each side so that I blocked her way.

It was brilliant. She couldn't look me in the eye. "I'm working here this summer, in the office." Words were tumbling out, she was so scared. "The others drink tea but I don't like it. I wanted something cold." Her fingers were twisting the soft green leather of the purse.

I laughed, liking the echoing sound it made, liking the way she flinched. "Elly, don't tell me you did something so bad they've got you working your butt off for the whole summer too."

"No!" Her voice was shrill, but she looked me straight in the face. "They advertised for a student to help update the tourist information. I applied and got the job."

Sneering, I swung forward, letting my arms take my weight, so I was right in her face. "Were you the only applicant?"

Her chin went up. "No, they interviewed five people before choosing me."

Snotty tone. Then I remembered how her old man had walked out a year ago, how her mother was weird. "So, they gave you the job because they felt sorry for you, eh? *Difficult family circumstances.*"

Tears started to show in her eyes. She turned and ran back up the corridor, heels clattering.

"Hey Elly," I called. "Changed your mind about that drink?" Grinning, I picked up my mop and got back to work, whistling to drown out the voices drifting in from outside.

Every day was the same. I reported in to Joe each morning, after ignoring the gauntlet of kids outside. Lister was always there, though his hangers-on changed. Must have been fairly boring coming to the community centre every morning and afternoon just to taunt me. Makes you wonder if he had anything else to do. It made a kind of warped sense — most people think I'm a real bad, wild kid so if he took me on he'd look tough. Kind of pathetic but drove me crazy.

I got more than enough yap from Brennan. Every hour he came in. Always found something to niggle about – a drip of paint on the floor, a bristle stuck in the paint on the wall. It was almost funny, because I *knew* how to paint. Used to help Gran. Joe said I was doing a good job, let me get on with it. But Brennan, he was something else. It was like he wanted me to lose my temper. Every day I nearly did, but I thought I still had a chance of going back to Toronto, so I stayed cool. Dad hadn't given me the big kiss-off speech yet about how Jenni the Jerk was pregnant and she couldn't become upset. Saved that news till I'd finished my community service, till I asked him. Used to imagine going for Brennan, though: jamming his head into the paint can, smacking the mop down on his head so hard that the handle broke. I hated him.

Just about the only person who didn't give me a hard time – not then, anyway – was Elly. Sweet Elly.

At least twice a day, Elly had to come through that big room I was working in. Sometimes it was to take files to the offices beyond, other times it was to get cans from the pop machine. Now that it was hot, the others in the front office had given up on tea. I used to wait for her, got a real kick out of the way she'd stand on the threshold, peering in from the shadows, trying to work out whether I'd notice if she tried to sneak by.

Once, I let her get halfway across the room before I spun around – smart, eh! Nearly fell off the ladder laughing. She literally jumped in the air and froze like one of those deer you catch in your headlights at night.

"Oh, Elly, did I scare you?"

"No. You startled me – that's all," she said uncertainly.

"Is that right? Jumpy, aren't you? Got bad nerves like your old lady? Hear she won't even go out of the house." It was almost too easy, the way she winced.

But Elly's voice sounded kind of defiant. "She's ill."

"Crazy is what I heard, only I was too polite to say – crazy as a loon. People say that's why your old man cut and ran." Eyed her up and down. She was shifting from foot to foot, like she was deciding whether to argue or make a run for it. Just looking at her told me she was seriously weird – skirt too long, plain blouse buttoned right up to the neck. Flat, ugly old-lady shoes. With a grin, I said, "Like mother, like daughter, eh?"

She stood real still then, clenched her hands. "Why are you always so horrible? What have I ever done to you?"

Made my face look as sad as I could. "Why, Elly, I don't know what you mean. I thought we were just having a friendly chat about family, and I seem to have upset you. Please accept my sincerest appy-polly-loggies." I bowed low, coming up laughing, but she was gone, stomping into the office. Didn't even look around when I shouted, "Don't hang around after work here. Mommy'll be waiting!"

I didn't like getting no reaction. Like, was I losing my touch? It was nearly time to pack up – five minutes by the wall clock – so I started to clean my brushes in the cupboard sink. With the water running, I didn't hear the footsteps.

"Slacking off, I see." Brennan had this shark-like grin.

I looked at the clock but he just stood there, pleased with himself. Went into this lecture about how poor time-keeping was symptomatic of my bad attitude. I could feel anger building up inside me like pop in a can that had been shaken up. Ten minutes after five he kept me, sneaking looks at his watch like he'd set himself some target. Must have washed that brush five times, just for something to focus on so I wouldn't say anything to him. Didn't trust myself not to blow up, lash out.

"Well, I suppose you'd better go. But in future you will wait until I tell you to go." This was dumb – obviously he'd made it up on the spot just to give me a hard time. Half the time he wasn't even there at five, out on some community crap.

"What if you're not here? Do I have to wait till you get back?" I couldn't keep the rage out of my voice.

"There's no need to take that tone with me, Bob." His grin got broader. "You ask Joe, of course."

I knew what Joe's reaction would be when I told him he was to be my jailer. "Ah, take no notice, boy. He talks a load of garbage, that one." That thought made me smile, but I kept my head down so Brennan couldn't see.

"Can I go now?"

Brennan looked around the room, trying to find something to criticize. "All right. Just make sure you don't try and take off early again." He didn't move from the doorway of the cupboard, so I had to squeeze past him.

I was seething when I hit the corridor, so mad I felt like punching the walls. The only good thing about being late was that the creep chorus outside might have gone home.

No such luck.

Lister was there with a couple of the others. The weird

thing was, one of them was Buddy Covington.

"Hey, Bob, got a friend of yours here!" Mark turned around, like he wanted the others to see how smart he was, how cool. Like I'm really going to be bothered by Buddy.

Kept on walking, didn't even show I'd heard, didn't move to the outside of the sidewalk to avoid them. Mark stepped to block me, and the others got up from the bench. Did a quick count – four. Two wouldn't do anything. Mark was the one to worry about, maybe Buddy. He was a scrawny little jerk, but he'd been picking on some of the younger kids lately – grade-school kids, would you believe.

"What's the matter? You in a hurry? No time to chat with your friends?" Mark looked eager. Buddy stepped up to his side, grinning.

I tried to shoulder past them, but Mark was expecting it. He leaned in towards Buddy and shoved me back.

"Think you're tough, don't you? You really look down on us like we're hicks or something." Mark was enjoying himself. He started pushing me, little jabs in time with his words.

The anger solidified into a hard lump. I'd had enough.

Quickly I checked that the street was empty, the lights off in the community centre. When Buddy stepped forward, gave me a tentative shove, I blew. I pushed Buddy aside, then moved in on Mark, kneeing him where it hurts. Just like clockwork: he doubled over and I head-butted him. Bone on bone. Then he fell to the ground.

"Well, you little snot-rag, you wanna try, too?" My fists were ready but Buddy backed away, trying to bury himself in the pair by the bench.

Looked down at Mark, smiled when I saw the blood

trickling from his nose. Couldn't resist. I leaned over, spat right in his face. "Share it with your gutless friends." Loud so they all heard. Then I moved off.

When I was a safe distance away, Mark shouted something, couldn't hear what. Might have been more impressive if he hadn't sounded like he was crying. That's right, I thought, keep going. He was all mouth. Now he'd be off my back.

Big mistake.

Nothing happened for a couple of days. The painting was almost done. Elly looked close to tears every time I spoke to her. Even C.J. had lightened up on me, admitted he hadn't thought I'd keep at it. I kinda liked that – proving him wrong, that is, not what he said.

It was a Thursday morning. I just had the woodwork to do, but didn't have the varnish yet, so I was touching up a few spots, getting splatters off the floor. Brennan sent for me, wanted to talk about the hours I still had to put in. He'd dreamed up some new scheme, changing one of the back offices into a day care for when they had ladies' badminton. Wanted me to help Joe with it. OK with me – Joe was all right. But I had to act out a bit. Couldn't disappoint my chum Alec.

"Oh, man, do I have to? Isn't there something I could do where I didn't have that old guy on my back all the time?"

Brennan's eyes gleamed. Rolled each word around his mouth like candy. "Bob, you should be grateful we're doing this for you. We've got to find suitable tasks. Anyway, Joe speaks quite highly of your work."

"Yeah, well, he would, wouldn't he? That room looks better now than it did before I messed it up. This is a good deal for you guys." Pushed my chair back hard, liking the noise it made and the way Brennan winced. As I walked out, I muttered, "Jerk" just right – loud enough so he knew I'd said something, too quiet for him to know what it was.

I was still working on the paint splatters when Joe came in.

"Bob, they've got a blood-donor clinic in the main hall at two. Come give me a hand setting out the chairs and unloading the stuff from the Red Cross trucks. You can finish up here later."

It was a change. Also gave me a chance to scare poor little Elly. Passed her as she was going to the back offices. Managed to knock into her and send her armful of folders flying. "Sorry, Elly, didn't see you there. Love to stay to help but gotta go with Joe." Got a real kick out of the way she glared at me.

Worked with Joe for about half an hour. It was outside, nice. Mark and his cronies were hanging around out front, but they just watched us. When Joe was in one of the trucks, I gave Mark the finger and a real cheesy grin. After a few minutes they took off, heading along the sidewalk, down past the parking lot.

The clinic organizer offered Joe and me coffee and cookies, so we were sitting at one of the tables when Brennan came tearing in like Dracula was after him. His face had gone almost purple. He grabbed me by the shoulders and hauled me out of my seat, shouting and spraying me with spit.

"You little creep! Your mother and her smart-ass lawyer friend won't get you off this time."

Wrenching free, I squared off to him. "What are you

talking about."

People had stopped what they were doing, staring at us, but Brennan didn't seem to care. He shoved me hard on the chest with both hands. "Don't give me any back talk. Just get to my office. I'm calling the police and your mother – in that order."

"I haven't done anything!" I was getting steamed. What gave him the right to push me around? I was going to take a swing at him if he touched me again – I just couldn't take it any more.

Joe stepped between us. "Bob, go with him. Try and sort this out, whatever it is." Stayed glaring at Brennan until Joe put a hand on my shoulder, lowered his voice and added, "Don't blow it now. You've only got one more week."

Brennan walked away. Everything was falling apart. I'd played their game, put up with everyone's crap. What was going on?

Brennan's office was at the front of the building, but he dragged me out a side door into the parking lot. Thought he was going to hit me now that there were no witnesses. Waited for him to throw that first punch.

It never came.

"Look! Just take a look!" He was sweating as he pulled me over to his car. He drove a white VW convertible with black leather seats. Didn't look so cool now. Thick gobs of green paint, the paint I'd been using, had been poured all over its inside.

"I didn't do that!" My heart was thudding and cold sweat was running down my neck. "Do you think I'm crazy? Why would I do something like that?"

"Why? Because you're a twisted little creep who lashes out when he doesn't get his own way. They threw you out of the youth club, so you vandalized their meeting room. You didn't like me telling you to work with Joe, so you did this!"

"I didn't. I swear I didn't." I was in big trouble now.

Brennan laughed, an ugly cracking sound. "You can do all the swearing you like for the police."

My legs felt like lead. Things were whirling around in my head. I just knew this was the end. Thought about how Mom would look when she came down here, about Jenni saying, "Well, what did you expect?"And Dad's silence.

In the office, I tried again. "Look, I was with Joe. Ask him. Someone's trying to get me into trouble. Those kids who hang out by the war memorial – they've got it in for me. They know everyone'll blame me." Hated how scared I sounded.

"You expect me to believe that crap! You had time. After you left my office. I know because I was the one who sent Joe to get you when the truck arrived." He had it all worked out. "So, just shut up. I don't want to listen to you. Sit down while I make those calls."

Flung myself down into a chair by the wall. Just as he was starting to dial, there was a knock at the door.

"What?" he yelled. "I'm busy."

The door opened a crack and Elly peered around. Her voice was small. "Mr. Brennan, I need to talk to you."

"Not now, Elly."

"It's about Bob, Mr. Brennan. It's important."

Great. Now she was coming in for the kill, tell Brennan

all about how I'd been teasing her. Didn't really blame her. I'd have done the same myself.

Sighing, Brennan motioned her to come in. "What else has he done?"

Elly slipped into the room, stood in front of Brennan's desk, pleating her skirt between her fingers. Didn't look at me. "I was going to the back office to do some filing when Joe and Bob were going over to the main hall." She paused. I figured she was trying to describe how I knocked into her, make it sound really bad.

Brennan was tapping his fingers impatiently on the phone. "Elly, what's this got to do with anything?"

She winced then, didn't look at him after that, just stared at the carpet. "While I was in the office I heard voices. I knew it wasn't Bob and Joe, so I looked out to see. It was Mark Lister and some other kids from school. They'd picked up one of the cans of paint, and when they saw me they ran." She sneaked a glance at me. "I thought that maybe they wanted to mess up the Bob's work and that I'd scared them off. It wasn't till Mrs. Denning told me about your car that . . . I knew . . . why they were really there."

Realized then that I'd stopped breathing while Elly was talking, saving my butt. Drew in a deep breath, ready to speak, to let Brennan have it but he beat me to it.

"Are you sure, Elly?" When she nodded, he turned to me. Swear he sounded disappointed. "I suppose this gets you off the hook. If it'd been anyone other than Elly, I'd have thought you two were in it together. You're lucky she spoke up for you. Why, I don't know. You're a nasty kid, seem determined to make people dislike you." Reaching for the phone, he stared at me. "There's always someone to bail you out, isn't there? Well, you're mine for the next week, so there's still plenty of time for you to screw up. I'm sure the police will want to speak to both of you. In the meantime, get back to what you were doing. Elly, you wait a moment."

Had to get out of there. Thought I was going to throw up. I stood with my back against the corridor wall, breathing deeply. Elly came out in a few minutes, stopped, looked at me.

"Are you all right?"

I wasn't. "Yeah."

She turned to go.

Wanted to speak but I didn't know what to say. I reached out, grabbed her arm. "Look, I'm so . . ." Never finished.

A look of disgust crossed her face. She shook her arm free and walked towards the main office.

Like I said, things have been weird lately. Since I finished at the community centre, Mom's given me some space. Told you how Dad gave me the kiss-off. He says I can come visit but I know he'll have even less time for me now, once the jerklet's born.

I've done a lot of thinking, mainly about Elly. Why did she speak up? And this morning, in the hall at school – why did she look like that? What does she think about? She's really driving me crazy.

About the Author

Gillian Chan trained as an English and Drama teacher. She taught for ten years in high schools and also worked as a school librarian. For the past six years, Gillian has lived in Dundas, Ontario. *Golden Girl and Other Stories* draws upon her experiences as a teacher and her love of books written for young adults. She has written a second collection of stories set in Elmwood, *Glory Days and Other Stories*.